US MARSHAL
HARRY FINCH

RENDEZVOUS WITH BOOT HILL

E. C. HERBERT

Cover Design by Outlaws Publishing LLC
Published by Outlaws Publishing LLC
July 2024
10987654321

PROLOGUE

US Marshal Harry Finch was once again on a mission, and that was to bring the notorious gunfighter, gun-for-hire, and just plain down-right murderer Slade Rawlins in to stand trial for the murder of Eva Wilcox, a well-known and liked singer, dancer and sometime prostitute who worked at Skinners Saloon. The wildest, whiskey-slinging drinking establishment in the lawless town of Cripple Creek, Colorado.

Slade Rawlins was a gun-for-hire and it didn't matter to him if you were a man, woman or child. If someone wanted you dead and had his price, well, consider yourself dead.

He had killed Eva in a fit of anger and drunkenness saying she had raffled his pockets and took his money, an acquisition which wasn't believed. He shot and killed the sheriff who went to arrest him. His ranch, which was about three miles west of Cripple Creek, became his hide-out and he surrounded himself with other known criminals.

Being wanted already and having a wanted poster out, the reward money was increased. Until US Marshal Harry Finch, better known as plain Finch, got the assignment to bring him in, no lawman, bounty hunter or other marshals were able to, or for that matter, willing to do so.

Many a grave in a town's Boot Hill cemetery was attributed to his guns. Many a cell in a state prison was attributed to Finch's tenacity to bring his subject to trial.

His latest assignment, bring in the notorious Slade Rawlings! An assignment he relished because it would mean there was one less bad guy free to hurt innocent folks.

BOOT HILL

Boot Hill was the name given to a section of most of the old western cemeteries where the less desirables were buried. Those being ramrods, gunfighters, and outlaws who were hanged or gunned down. Some of those whose names were known had a marker, but most graves there were marked by a simple pile of rocks. The name Boot Hill was in reference to the fact they all died with their boots on.

Some of the famous more well-known Boot Hill cemeteries are located in: Tombstone, Arizona, Dodge City, Kansas, Deadwood, South Dakota, Virginia City, Nevada, and Idaho City, Idaho.

Today, all are opened to the public and can be visited online.

CHAPTER 1

US Marshal Harry Finch had been with the Agency for ten years. In that period of time, he excelled in every area he was assigned and would be considered a professional in some fields.

Finch's dad was a US Marshal and for as long as he could remember as a kid, he wanted to follow in his footsteps. So his dad did everything he could to always live up to the standards and motto of the US Marshals. Harry was doing everything hc could to do the same, but at the start it was tough. Being the son of such a highly respected member of the US Marshals, he was expected to excel in all assignments he was given.

Two days ago, Finch received a package from the Agency. Inside was a folder that contained the file information on a gunman, murderer named Slade Rawlins, and today he was on his way to a town named Cripple Creek, which was the last place he'd been seen.

Since the US Marshaling Agency was conceived by George Washington during his Presidency, the Agency has been keeping files and records on most outlaws and criminals.

The hot, dusty, never ending bumping, jarring, rickety ride of the overland stage coach, as it made its way over the never ending deep ruts in a one horse trail was starting to get to him. Normally, he would be in his private railroad car, but needed to get his body used to this kind of travel again. There were no tracks going to most of the western areas he would be going to on this assignment. From here on in until this mission was over, it would be stage coach and horseback and living out under the stars and his body had grown weak from lack of this kind of activity.

There were three other passengers on the stage. The Johnson sisters, Lillian and Prentice, who, by the way they were dressed, had to be Soiled Doves, this just one of the many names given to the prostitutes of the day, and a gentlemanly dressed passenger who called himself, Sam Colter.

Finch, who was always studying files and had a photographic mind, remembered reading that name, and now he brought it up from the libraries of his mind.

Sam Colter was a Bounty Hunter from the east whose reputation was to only go after those who had bounties on their heads of five hundred dollars or more, and were wanted dead or alive. His file showed he had never brought anyone in alive, so he was branded with the name of Sammy, the Bring'em in Dead Bounty Hunter.

Since boarding this stage, no one had spoken a word so Finch's mind was screaming to be fed with new information which it was always doing, more so when his surroundings were lived first hand.

"You have quite the reputation, Mr. Colter," said Harry, wanting to find out all he could from this bounty hunter.

"I could say the same about you, US Marshal Harry Finch."

Harry picked up a tone of animosity in his voice and wondered how a bounty hunter could possibly know about him.

"How do you know me?" asked Harry.

"C'mon Finch!" Sam exclaimed. "Ain't that photographic mind of yours working?"

Suddenly, information surfaced and Finch said out loud. "Randy, Randy Shelton."

"I was wondering how long that was gonna take, Harry," he said. "Is your memory getting slow, or just plain old like you? I recognized your face as soon as you boarded the stage."

"That's because I didn't know that Randy Shelton and Sam Colter were one in the same. When you left the Agency, your name dropped off the face of the earth. What happened to you, anyways?" Harry asked, although he already knew his answer as his memory had brought up all information he had on him, but wanted to hear it from him.

"Pretty simple, Finch. I got tired of tracking down the bad guy and not getting anything in return, so when my wife got sick and I needed money for her doctors, I knew what I had to do to get it. I quit the Agency, changed my name then went out and found my first bounty." Thinking back on all that now, he continued.

"That first bounty, Finch, was a thousand dollars! The tone in his voice changed as well as his facial features as he continued.

"I didn't kill him like I was accused of doing, Finch," he told him. "He fell off his horse and broke his neck. You know what, Harry? They still paid me the thousand dollars."

Noticing the two women were looking at him with uneasy looks, he said to them.

"Don't worry about me ladies, unless of course, you have a price on those pretty little heads of yours."

Both girls shook their heads.

"Good, then. You have nothing to worry about from me," he told them with a big grin on his face. Turning back to Finch, he continued his story.

"As I was saying, I still collected the thousand-dollar reward. I never gave a thought to not bringing a wanted person in other than alive, till my next bounty," he continued. "He was wanted for the rape of a young girl. On the trail, he broke loose and attacked me, so I shot him in self-defense. Right then and there I saw that if a person was dead, I had nothing to fear, plus I didn't have to feed him. So I only went after those wanted dead or alive. You know my reputation of always bringing them in strapped laying across the saddle." Sam's reference to the dead man.

"We at the Agency don't look too highly on that, you having been a marshal and all."

"I don't care what you and the Agency think, Finch. I'm not breaking any laws. I do have the right to defend myself."

"Just keep it that way and we'll stay good. Break that law and you become no different than the ones you hunt down, except you'll have me on your trail."

"Sounds threating, Finch! I don't take to threats very well."

"Then don't take it as a threat, but a promise," said Finch.

Finch saw, as well as heard, the difference in Sam's tone of voice and decided to end the conversation with him fearing it might escalate into something other than conversation.

Turning toward the two ladies, Finch nodded and asked, "Who does my friend Sam and I have the pleasure of traveling with? It's not often you see two ladies dressed like you two traveling by stage."

"Why, thank you. Marshal Finch is it?"

"Yes it is, but Harry will do."

"Okay. Harry it will be," she said. "I'm Lillian and this is my sister Prentice, we're known as the Johnson sisters and we sing and dance. We're headed to Kansas City where we will meet up with two more and then take the train to Denver."

As she spoke, Finch had a strange feeling come over him and decided these two needed to be watched closely.

Before they knew it, they had arrived at Nappy Smith's Overland Express Station. Nappy's had been a Pony Express change-off station. Now it was a trading post and stop off place for the few stage coaches still in operation.

Nappy had a reputation of welcoming all travelers with a halfway decent stew, hot coffee and biscuits and a decent bunkhouse. There was some kind of Indian made beverage that those who had drank of it would advise against it for health reasons. That is, if you drink it, you fall down and hurt yourself.

Upon entering Nappy's, you were met by an old Indian Squaw who couldn't speak and walked with a very bad limp. Story had it, she showed up one day and never left. Nappy called her old woman and that name stuck.

As soon as everyone had something to eat, it was bedtime. Traveling by stage was not an easy method of travel. It was hard on one's body, and unlike traveling horseback where you could stop from time to time, once the stage was moving, it stayed moving, stopping only to water and feed the team, then you had a few minutes to disembark and stretch your legs.

Daylight would come before you knew it, and the stage would leave as soon as the team was fed and hitched up, regardless if you were ready or not.

After eating, Harry went outside to walk around and do some thinking on the previous day's happenings.

Randy had been a good Deputy US Marshal right up until the start of his wife's illness, then he started to change. It was obvious his whole existence was built around his wife, who he was very private about. He never mentioned her by name, or ever had anyone over to their house or going to anyone else's.

Randy's work started to suffer. He became confrontational with his superiors and was always complaining about pay and how they should be awarded any money that was offered for the criminals they had to bring in. He was written up several times and when his wife passed, he quit. Shortly after he quit, he brought in his first bounty, dead.

His story wasn't believed and he stood trial, but was acquitted. After that, he dropped out of sight. Many believed he must be dead.

"Now, I know you aren't dead. You simply changed your name and moved away," Harry spoke into the darkness. Harry had a restless night sleep having woken several times by what he thought were voices and light footsteps, but closed his eyes and went back to sleep.

Now Harry was again woken up by the sounds of men's voices and the neighing, snorting sounds of horses, along with the clip-clop of their footsteps.

"Stage leaves in twenty minutes, folks," came a voice from outside.

The old woman had some breakfast on the table and there was a large pot of coffee on the stove. Finch acknowledged the presence of Sam, but wondered where the Johnson sisters were.

"Let's board up!" exclaimed the gruff voice of the stage driver.

Finch hollered up to the driver.

"The two women who were on the stage yesterday. They're not here yet," he informed the driver.

"And they won't be," it was Nappy and he told him that the two ladies had rented a wagon and had left right at dawn.

"Where did they rent the wagon to?" he asked Nappy.

"Freidman Junction. It's another trading post about a hundred miles north," he told Finch. "I tried to talk them out of it cause the trail gets really rough and not really fit for a wagon, but they insisted and paid me twice what I asked for."

"What are your thoughts, Harry?"

It was Randy's voice. He had walked up behind him and heard his conversation with Nappy.

"Well, they surely weren't dressed to do that kind of traveling," he answered him.

"That's where you're mistaken, my friend," said Nappy. "They swapped their dresses for some old buckskins I had out back. Sold them my old ten-gauge double barreled shotgun also."

"Now what do you make of that?" asked Sam.

"You're sounding like a marshal there, Randy," said Finch. "It's no concern for either of us, unless, of course, you have some business with them?"

"Sam! Harry! The name is Sam. Remember that," he said. "And you're right, don't concern me one bit."

"Stage's leaving!" exclaimed the driver, climbing into the driver's seat. "Get in or get out of the way, choice is yours."

Driver wasn't kidding. As soon as he heard the stage door close, it leaped forward as the driver whistled and snapped the reins in the air causing the four hitched team to bolt forward. Slamming both, Harry and Sam against the rear wall of the stage.

As the stage rambled along, Finch couldn't help thinking something wasn't right where the Johnson sisters were concerned, and the gnawing he was feeling in the pit of his stomach, told him their paths would cross again.

Finch's mind was a jumbled mass of unanswered questions starting with the Johnson sisters and who were they? Why were they on this particular stage? Why leave in such a mysterious way? Why didn't they ask more questions of him and Sam, once they knew who they were? After all, they are women, but instead, actually became quieter as if they didn't want to call attention to themselves.

The stage rambled on and every now and then hit a deep rut or hole and Finch and Sam were tossed around inside the coach like rag dolls.

"What in tar nation is the matter with that driver?" Finch said, having been tossed into the air in a violent bout with an extra deep rut in this horse trail.

The morning stage ride had been really rough and Finch's thoughts were as jumbled up as the rest of him was physically, so he welcomed the sound of Sam's voice.

"I know that look, Finch. What are your thoughts on me or those two ladies?"

"Both." answered Finch. "But more on them at the present. I can't shake the feeling that they aren't who they say they are."

"Well, let me shine a little light on your darkness," he answered. "And I'm doing it out of respect for you, not the Agency. I could care less about them, but you! I've heard your name mentioned and those stories I've heard told, if only are half true, well, they in themselves warrant respect."

Sam became quiet for a minute and looked out onto the terrain and shook his head ever so slowly.

"If only I'd stuck it out."

"You can always come back," said Finch. "You were making your mark there at the start, but at the end, well, you know. You don't need me dragging up all that crap again and opening old wounds."

"Thanks. To get back to what we started. You're right in questioning who the Johnson sisters are, because they aren't the Johnson sisters."

Sam noticed, Finch's raised eyebrows and knew he had sparked an interest.

"Their real names are Delores and Bridget Avery." Sam told him. "There is a thousand-dollar bounty on each of them."

Finch's mind reacted to the names in less than a heartbeat.

"They're wanted for coach robbery and for jail break," Finch told Sam. "I wonder what they're doing in this part of the country." Finch hoped that Sam would shine some light where they were concerned.

"They usually operate in and around Oklahoma and Texas," Sam told Finch. "Things have been heating up down there which has forced them to move to a different area," Sam decided to share some more information with Finch and maybe he might learn something about the whereabouts of several wanted outlaws. After all, US Marshal Harry Finch would only be in this part of the country, if he was picking up someone to bring back east, or looking for someone that no one else had been able to find or take in.

"This was the closest I've come to them, since I picked up their trail in Oklahoma."

"Well. That answered my question of why you, a bounty hunter, would be traveling by way of stage coach."

"I'm not your typical bounty hunter, Finch. Where I used to apprehend the crook, now I follow them to see if they meet up with another wanted person. That way I have been able to collect more bounties. Take those Avery sisters. There is no way they have been acting alone. They had to have an accomplice who they tie up with."

Another rut had Sam sticking his head out the coach's window and yelling up to the driver he was going to blow his head off, if he wasn't more careful with his driving.

"I talked with a coach driver down in Oklahoma City who had been held up by those two and he told me there was a third person. That person, being a guy, wearing a poncho and acted like he was the leader, giving orders and all. Only person I have ever known to wear a poncho is the gunman Slade Rawlins."

"What would a gunman like Slade Rawlins be doing holding up a stage coach? Doesn't make no sense to me," Harry said after a moment's thought. "Why would Slade be involved in stage robbery? He's a gunman and killer, not a stage robber?" he repeated. "And in Oklahoma? He is usually in Colorado and the mid-west."

Harry contemplated telling Sam that he was searching for him, but decided not to.

"Interesting isn't it Finch," Sam remarked.

"How come you're not following those sisters now?" Harry asked Sam.

"Well, Finch. They're headed to Freidman Junction, which I would venture means they will be boarding the train for Colorado, and that's where this coach is headed. I think they got spooked when they found out you were a US Marshal and I was a bounty hunter."

"Why didn't you grab them at Nappy's?" Finch asked him.

"As I told you earlier, I was waiting to see where they went and who they might meet. If they had something going on with Slade, why that's another well worth bounty."

The coach hitting another deep rut threw both Sam and Harry into the air which drew a loud response from Sam.

"You're about to meet your maker, driver!" he said in a loud voice, giving Harry a big smile at the same time.

CHAPTER 2

"That was a close one," said Bridget to her sister Delores.

The buckboard wagon they had rented from Nappy that morning hit a deep rut in the trail and both sister's bottoms lost contact with the seat coming down a second later with two loud "ummmmphs."

"Not much better than the stage was," Delores remarked, grabbing hold of the metal rail that surrounded the seat to help hold herself down. The folded horse blanket offering little padding for the hardwood seat.

"I'm glad those two on the stage started talking, if they hadn't we would probably be dead right now," Delores remarked. "Do you think they're following us?"

"They could be, but I doubt it," Bridget told her sister.

The happenings of the previous day had changed a lot of things for the two sisters. First, the stage they were on and planning to hold-up in order to get the money box that they knew was on that stage and contained some gold. But more important was the five thousand dollars in cold, hard cash. Money they were going to use to pay Wade Rawlings for his services.

Now, not only were they going to lose out on that money, but also the money they had to spend on the wagon, clothes, and shotgun.

"I hope they have a telegraph office in Freidman Junction, so we can get a message off to Wade," Bridget told her sister.

Dolores hardly heard her sister, she was so deep in thought. The constant jarring of the wagon along with its creaking noises made it more difficult for her to think straight.

"We need to stop for a few, so I can gather my thoughts together," she told her sister. "Looks like there might be a good place up ahead."

The place that Dolores spotted was indeed a good place to stop. It was plain to see, it had been used by many a traveler. There was a fire pit someone had built and lined with stones. Several large tree sections had been laid across two large rocks making a bench seat to sit on. Bridget spied a well-worn path and told her sister who had just sat down.

"There is a path over here," she called out to her sister. "I'm gonna follow it and see where it leads."

"Well, be careful. Let me know what you find," Dolores told Bridget, who was already far enough away that she didn't hear her.

The path was indeed well worn. Soon she came upon a spot that, judging from the smell, had been used by many as an outdoor outhouse. Hurrying past, she came to a small overhang with a creek running by it, and for a moment thought the place looked beautiful.

Bridget walked over to the creek that had been dammed up to create a small pool. Seeing the water was clear, she knelt down on a well-placed rock that obviously someone had moved there just for that reason. She was just about to cup some water up to splash onto her hot, sweaty face, when she caught her reflection in the water. Although her crystal, clear, reflection showed a beautiful woman's face, it was like this pool allowed her, for the first time in the previous year, to see herself on the inside, and she didn't particularly like what she saw.

Since her rape by Charles Freeman, she had put on a happier face than the one staring back at her now. The youthful, wrinkle free face that always had a smile on it was replaced by an older, wrinkled face that wore a look of sadness.

"Who is this woman's face looking back at me from this pool?" she said to herself. Her blueberry colored eyes, now almost black with horror, remembering her ordeal and the humiliation she went through because of who Charles Freeman was and the trial that followed.

Charles Freeman was on the City Council in Pleasant Pines, Colorado which was a bustling mecca of shops, hotels, saloons, dance halls, and gambling establishments on the trail from Denver to Deadwood, South Dakota.

"Bridget! Where are you?" it was Delores calling.

"I'm down by this creek," she answered back. "Follow the path and you will see for yourself."

Bridget thought for a moment about warning her sister of the outdoor outhouse area, but decided she needed a laugh and what better way to get one than at her sister's expense, and she didn't have to wait long.

"Oh my god, what's that horrible smell?" she heard her sister screech.

Bridget was still all smiles when Delores reached the creek.

"Why didn't you warn me?" she yelled at her sister.

"That was disgusting."

The outburst of laughter from her sister, quickly had her laughing to.

"Wow! What a beautiful spot." Delores exclaimed, looking around. Her eyes settling on the glass like pool of crystal clear water.

"Come over here." Bridget said to her sister, motioning to her with a flailing arm. As she approached, Bridget moved aside so that her sister could kneel on the rock. "Look into the water," she told her sister. "The water is so clear, it's like looking into a mirror."

"Indeed it is," said Delores, looking at her reflection in the pool, framed by the blue sky and white, cotton candy clouds which painted the backdrop above that reflection.

Realizing they must be going, Delores stood and told her sister they needed to be making dust, if they were to reach the settlement of Eastman that Nappy had told them about. Knowing what was coming, both sisters reached up and pinched their noses shut then quickened their steps when they reached the smelly, outdoor outhouse area.

"Miss us?" Bridget looked down and asked the seat in a sarcastic voice, as she and her sister climbed aboard and sat down once again.

A loud clicking of her tongue, followed by the snapping sound of the leather reins above the horse's back, and once again they were under way. Neither sister spoke for some time. Instead, they rode in silence, taking in the ever present creaking of the buckboard and the clip-clop sound of the horse's hooves stepping on the hard packed trail.

There was a slight breeze singing a song as it made its way through the tree branches and evergreens. The cawing of a crow, warning of approaching danger.

A few miles down the road Delores asked, "My, you're awfully quiet. What are you thinking about?"

Once again, the wagon lurched skywards when one of its front wheels confronted a rut in the trail and lost, sending both girls into the air.

"Ummmmph!" was heard again from the skyward bound women as they fell back to earth and their bottoms landing on the not-so-well-padded buckboard seat.

"I was about to say. Back there at the pool, I saw my reflection in the water and I didn't like the person I have become," she answered. Correcting her statement, she repeated, "What we've become."

"What do you mean, what we've become?" her sister asked.

"You know! Stage robbers! Whores!" she exclaimed. "Now look at us! We're going to hire a gunman to murder someone. And for money!" Her voice, high pitched again, and on the verge of breaking down. Delores looked over at her sister and saw her eyes water over, then run down her cheek.

"We've become who we are in order to survive!" her sister exclaimed. "We needed to get away from home when we did, it was as simple as that," Delores replied. "Neither of us would have survived. We do, what we do, to survive."

"I know," replied Bridget. "And I'm forever thankful that you took control and got us out of there. I was just feeling sad for myself. I thought at this stage in my life I'd be married, have children, be cooking, sewing, taking care of my own little farm. Who knows? I might have even been a school teacher."

The tone in her voice and the look on her face became softer as she told her sister what was on her mind.

"Whoa," Delores said to the horses, pulling back on the reins.

Bringing the wagon to a stop, Delores reached over and invited her sister into her outstretched arms. Bridget welcomed the hug from her sister and fell into her arms.

"Ummmmm!" she purred, feeling the warm, secure embrace from her sister, as she wrapped her arms around her and cradled her head against her bosom so that she even heard the beating of her sister's heart. For a moment, she pictured herself in her sister's place, coddling her own child. The feeling they both had at that moment needed no words.

The air around them was still. The only sounds were the low nickering, neighing noises from the horses and the creaking of the seat as Delores gently rocked her sister in her arms. It had been some time since either one of them had felt this closeness they were enjoying now, and neither wanted the moment to end, but end it must.

Bridget felt the light patting of her sister's hand in the center of her back and the low whispered, "Time we best be moving on if we are going to reach Eastman before dark," Delores said in a quiet voice.

Bridget felt her sister slowly unwrap her embrace.

"Thanks, Delores."

"I love you, little sister," Delores told her. "Everything's going to be alright."

The horses, who had been waiting patiently, welcomed the clicking of the tongue and the snap of the reins signaling it was time to get a move on. And as a reminder to the sisters that the trip was far from over, one of the wagon's wheel dropped into a rut, thus, once again sending them heaven bound, only to drop them back down with a loud, "Ummmmph" as bottom's made contact with the hard wagon seat. Rounding a bend in the trail, the two saw the first building of Eastman.

"Nappy sure was right when he said there's nothing much here," Delores said. "Oh, look! A saloon."

Sure enough, out of the handful of buildings, one had a big old sign hanging by two rusted lengths of chain with hand painted black letters that simply said, SALOON.

Bridget noticed the bullet holes in the sign, along with several in the front wall, and wondered just what kind of place this settlement, known as Eastman, was. The raised second story boardwalk or porch told her there were rooms above the saloon. Bridget also noticed there weren't very many people on the street, which wasn't unusual seeing what time of day it was.

"Let's go in and see if they have a room," Delores remarked. "Hopefully, a bath."

Pulling up in front of the saloon, both heard the loud rag-time beat coming from a piano. The rumble, an audible noise of a bunch of cowboys having a good time.

"Ready to go inside?" Delores asked, stepping down from the wagon. Once her two feet hit the dirt, she reached behind herself and gave her bottom a vigorous rubbing.

"My backside will never be the same," she said between rubs.

"I hear that!" exclaimed Bridget. Her feet, just landing on the street, sending a dull pain through her backside.

Stepping through the saloon's bat wing doors, the first thing they were confronted with was the smoke filled air followed by the sounds one heard in a western drinking establishment.

"Gosh dang! I've missed this kind of place," Bridget said, letting herself take it all in.

Sitting at one of the tables with three other cowboys, two of which had scantily dressed women sitting on their laps, looked in their direction and gave them the up and down look, stopping so they were looking eye to eye. Their look was threatening and for an instant Bridget was gonna tell her sister, let's get out of here, when the cowboy who had his back to them, turned around.

"Oh!" escaped from Bridget's lips, as their eyes met.

"What?" questioned Delores. Turning to see what brought the "oh" from her. At the same time, she felt Bridget's hand grasp her arm.

Looking in the direction of her sister's stare, Delores whispered questioning, "Dusty Robert?"

As they both watched, this cowboy stood up and turning, walked in their direction.

"It's Dusty, isn't it?" whispered Delores.

Not answering her sister, but letting go of her arm, Bridget stepped forward to meet an old friend, and mentor to them both, Dusty Roberts.

As Dusty arrived in front of them, he removed his big, white hat, ran his fingers through his coal black hair and said, "My oh my! If it isn't the two Avery sisters," he remarked.

The three stood starring at each other before wrapping their arms around themselves and greeting each other with a big hug, right there in the center of the saloon, in a hole-in-the-wall town known as Eastman. Dusty motioned for them to go get a table. He walked back to where he was sitting in a card game and started collecting his winnings.

One of the cowboys, obviously upset by his pulling out of the game, stood up suddenly and kicked his chair out from behind him and went for his sidearm. This error he would not live to regret. Even before his dead eyes could see the puff of smoke from Dusty's ivory gripped forty-five, an ounce of lead had entered his forehead ending his life and gambling days forever.

Even before he crumbled to the floor, the ivory gripped forty-five spun in the direction of the other two who were in the process of standing and reaching for their own shooters.

Dusty, shaking his still smoking forty-five at the two told them. "You can live or you can die. The choice is all yours, boys. There is plenty of room in Boot Hill for you two, right next to him."

Staring down the bore of a smoking forty-five and seeing brain matter mixed with hair, blood, and bone splattered on the wall right next to you from the man whose still warm body lays on the floor at your feet, and the acidy smell of exploded gunpowder invading your nostrils, not to mention the ringing in your ears from being on the front end of a gigantic, boooooom! Well, that all has a way of testing a man. The test of life versus death. With the situation at hand, time to pull up stakes, walk away, and live to enjoy another day!

The room had become deadly quiet with all eyes on the three. The two dance hall girls had moved away. As everyone watched, the two rough-necks moved their hands away from their holsters.

"Not our fight, mister."

As quickly as it had begun, it was over. The room suddenly came alive with the piano, sending its rag-time music into the room along with the sounds of regular folks enjoying themselves with women, cards and drink. Dusty had holstered his firearm, gathered his winnings off the table, and headed over where the sisters stood next to a table, but hadn't sat down.

Tipping his hat at the two, Dusty said, "You'll have to excuse me, ladies, but there are times when business over-rides pleasure. And now that the business has been taken care of, time for that pleasure. What would you two like to drink?"

CHAPTER 3

It hadn't been that long since Delores and Bridget last had contact with Dusty, but a lot of things had happened in that short period of time. Now, the three were once again enjoying drink, conversation and laughter together. Having just killed a man had no lasting effect on Dusty. As a matter of fact, it had none, which was obvious by the laughter coming from him as he enjoyed getting reacquainted with the two of them.

"So, tell me, what brings you two to Eastman?" then giving them the once over added, "And dressed like that!"

"Bridget and I had some business to attend to, but the plans fell through. So we're headed to Freidman Junction, then we will take the train to Cripple Creek where we have other business to take care of. After that?" she answered, tipping her hands palms up and hunching her shoulders.

"What about you?" she asked. Well aware he wasn't going to settle for her vague answer. They had spent enough time together for her to think he wouldn't want to know exactly what that business was.

"What brings you to this hole-in-the-wall place?" she asked.

Before he could reply, the town's sheriff walked in. He had no doubt been summoned concerning the shooting.

"The sheriff just walked in," she informed the others.

As Delores watched, he walked over to where the dead cowboy lay on the floor. She didn't hear him talking to the others, but she did see one of them point in their direction, to which he tipped his hat and turned and moved in their direction.

"Sheriff's walking over," she whispered, warning the others.

"Evening folks," he announced arriving at their table.

"Evening sheriff," all three answered in return.

"Mind filling me in as to what happened here tonight?"

"Happy to, sheriff," replied Dusty.

Dusty told his story and it became obvious he had acted in self-defense, besides there were plenty of witnesses to swear he had. Being satisfied there was no criminal act, the sheriff excused himself and told the barkeep he would be sending over a couple men to get the body.

"So! Now that excitement is over, I'll answer your question you had asked. I'm on the way to Colorado and a city named Cripple Creek."

"What a hoot!" Bridget stated. "That's where we were headed before our travel was interrupted by a bounty hunter and a US Marshal."

Delores noticed a change in Dusty's expression at the mention of a bounty hunter and Marshal.

Bridget continued, "We were on the stage when these two started chatting. Seems they knew each other years ago. As a matter of fact, the bounty hunter was an ex-US Marshal."

Once again, Delores caught a change in Dusty's facial expression and kncw shc had sparked some kind of interest.

"Do you recall their names?" he asked. Dusty leaned back in his seat, took a sip of his drink, and waited for Bridget to answer.

"How could anyone forget the names of those who had cost us five thousand dollars," she answered Dusty. "The US Marshal was Harry Finch and the bounty hunter was Sam Colter."

"Sam Colter," he repeated the name. The tone in his voice told Delores Dusty knew the name.

"You know who he is?" she asked.

"Ya! I know Sam. What I don't know, is why would he be traveling with this US Marshal?

"I don't think they were traveling together," Delores answered. "I think they were just on the same stage headed in the same direction."

Re-calling what Bridget said, Dusty asked, "How did these two cost you five-thousand dollars? That's a lot of dough," he remarked. Curiosity sounded in his voice.

"We overheard that a shipment of cash and gold was going out on the stage coach for Cripple Creek. When we saw them loading the strong box, we bought passage planning on holding it up. The driver and stage hand wouldn't be expecting two women dressed in fine clothes to be of any concern. Then we would wait till they made a rest stop, then overtake them, strip them naked, tie them up, and steal the whole darn coach."

"What about Sam and the marshal?" Dusty interrupted. "What were you intending on doing with them? You don't think they would just stand around, while you stripped the driver and shotgun naked. Do you? And why would a bounty hunter and a US Marshal be traveling on that stage?"

"We asked ourselves that same question. We figured that Sam must have been on our trail and was waiting for us to show our hand, then when we did, well! Everyone knows his reputation, so at the first overnight stop, we purchased a few things, rented a wagon and high-tailed it out of there."

"You're telling me that there is five thousand dollars in the stage's strong box?"

"That's right. We watched them load it. After all, we learned from the best." Bridget told him and reached over and touched his arm.

"Okay you two. Bridget, you amaze me! Dusty here, walked out on you when you needed him the most. And here you are…."

"Wait just one doggone, minute!" exclaimed Dusty. Daggers showing in his eyes and venom spurting from his lips.

"When Freeman stood trial and was found innocent, there was nothing more that I wanted than to see him dead for what he did to Bridget," looking directly at Bridget.

Then over to Delores, he said in a lower voice, "I loved you then Bridget, and I still love you, but Delores wanted me to gun Freeman down in cold bloody murder and I weren't about to do that. I don't suppose back then I could have shot no man. That's why I taught you two how to rob a stage coach without having to shoot anyone."

Dusty stopped talking for a moment before reaching out and taking Bridget's hand.

"I'm sorry. As much as I loved you and despised Freeman, I just couldn't take another man's life like that.

I felt like a coward and I let you down, so I left. No good-byes. Just got on my horse and rode away."

"Well, just so you know, I haven't changed my opinion of you, probably never will," Delores told him straight up. "As far as Freeman goes, I still want him dead and buried for what he did to Bridget. That rapist needs to be where he can't rape no one ever again."

"I told you, Sis. I've put that behind me and have moved on. You need to, also."

"What! What are you saying! Right up till five minutes ago when you saw Dusty again, you were all for us hiring this gunman Slade Rawlins and paying him to kill Freeman."

"I changgg---," before she could say another word, Dusty butted in.

"Slade Rawlins! You're looking to hire Slade Rawlins?"

"That's right. Slade Rawlins. Why? You know him?" Delores asked seeing Dusty's reaction to the name of Slade Rawlins.

"Ya! I know him. Carried around an ounce of lead from him before I found a doctor who dug it out. Do I know him? Ya! I know him."

"Why would he shoot you, Dusty?" asked Bridget.

Before he answered Bridget, Dusty scanned the room looking from one person to the next.

"Who you looking for?" asked Bridget.

"Just a habit I guess," he answered. "Rawlins has a pretty high bounty on his head. I tried to collect that bounty once and collected an ounce of his lead instead."

A look of astonishment came over both Delores and Bridget's faces upon hearing what Dusty just confessed to.

"You're a bounty hunter?" they both said at the same time, not believing what they had just heard.

"Shuuuuuurrr!" he indicated with a finger across his lips. "I don't want everyone to know who I am. I stop off here often and gather information on some of the desperadoes I'm hunting. If they knew who I really was, they would tighten up like a steel trap, or worse. Those other two at that table just now! Well they hate bounty hunters. They would ambush me or shoot me in the back. Wouldn't matter to them. One way or another, I'd end up in Boot Hill."

"How did you come about being a bounty hunter? You never was one to look for trouble. Or killing another man?"

Both Bridget and Delores had slid to the front of their chairs to lean in closer to hear what Dusty had to say.

"After the trial when I left, I went to Texas. I just wanted to get away from here and figured that was a far enough away place," a big sip of beer, then Dusty continued.

"I held up a couple stages on my way there and for the first time I had to gallop away empty handed when a passenger started shooting at me."

"Did you get hit?" Bridget asked. She had reached over and once again taken his hand in hers and was rubbing it between her fingers.

"Nope!" he exclaimed.

"Did you finally make it to Texas?" asked Delores. "What was Texas like? I've heard so many tales about the Texas cowboys. We were thinking about heading there after our business with Slade is done, unless we decide to stay in Colorado or even continue on to San Francisco."

At the mention of Slade's name, Delores saw Dusty's expression change and started to ask him about Slade, but Dusty spoke with continuation of his story.

"I tried one more time to hold-up a stage. Guess what!" he stated, shaking his head. "That strong-box was actually bolted down to the roof of the stage and had a big-ole-lock on it. Imagine that!"

"What did you do then?" Bridget asked with an excited voice.

"Only thing I could do. I needed money and if I couldn't get it from that strong-box, well, there were the passengers."

The two sisters were surprised to learn Dusty had actually robbed the passengers. After all, he had always preached against it.

"If you rob a passenger," he told them, "that person would be more apt at remembering your face, so you never did that. You were to avoid as much contact with the passengers as you could, and if confronted in any way that was threatening to you where you might want to return that threat, then you rode away as fast as your mount would take you."

Delores was remembering all of that now, as she listened to him tell them what he had been up to since leaving.

"After that last hold-up, I made up my mind that stage robbing was nothing I would do again. I had a long trail ride and plenty of time to think about what I was going to do next."

"I had forgotten how pretty Bridget's eyes were. And her smile! Dusty thought as he sat there telling his tales. "I need to talk to her without her sister around."

"Finish your story." It was Bridget's voice that brought him back from his thoughts.

"Texas was hot and dry and there didn't seem to be any place where there wasn't dust in the air to fill up your nose and cake onto your sweaty face. I knew that riding the range wasn't a life-long job for me."

"Why, seeing the way you're dressed and that wad of money you picked up off the table, I'd say you're a gambler, plus that other thing."

"Right on both counts. I started out playing cards and found I was quite good at it. Anyways, one day this fella came into the saloon. I had just sat down and dealt out a hand, when he turned with his back to the bar facing all in the room and, holding up a wanted poster with a man's face on it, asked if anyone had seen him. When no one answered him, he stepped over to my table and grabbing ahold of the table's edge, flung it through the air along with our cards, money, and drinks."

"Wow! What happened next?" asked Bridget.

She hadn't realized it but she was squeezing Dusty's hand tightly, as she listened to the build-up to the story.

"When I saw him head towards my table with his glaring eyes on me, I drew my sidearm out and had it in my lap when the table went flying, exposing it. If he would have stopped, that would have been the end of it all," he said, motioning for another round of drinks for them.

"Maybe it was instinct, but when he saw my pistol, he went for his, leaving me no choice but to fire. My bullet entering his belly and exiting his back, taking out his backbone as it did."

"You killed a man?" asked Bridget.

With a sad look on his face, and the slight nod of his head was all that needed to be said.

"Have you had to kill anyone else?" This time it was Delores who asked the question.

Turning at the sound of some commotion in the room, all three watched as two men picked up the body of the dead man and carried him out.

Turning back around, and making eye contact with Delores, Dusty simply stated. "Answer your question?"

As the drinks flowed, more tales were told by them all and it was becoming quite clear to Delores that her sister was once again falling for the handsome Dusty.

"Before it gets any later, we need to find us a room for the night. A bath and some supper would be nice also."

Getting up from the table, Dusty excused himself.

"I'll be right back," he told them. They watched as he walked up to the bartender and stood talking for a few minutes. They watched as the bartender reached under the bar and came up with a key which he placed on the bar top in front of Dusty.

"Looks like Dusty is getting us a room." Bridget mentioned to her sister.

"Looks that way," she replied. "And a nice hot bath, I hope."

Returning to the table, Dusty handed Delores the room key and a round red metal token.

"That's good for two hot baths that will be ready in about half an hour. Just give it to the old Mexican woman down at the bath house. She'll take care of you."

"What do we owe you?" asked Delores. She had started opening her purse when he replied.

"It's on me. Just enjoy. I'll catch up with you later, let's say eight o'clock right back here and I'll buy you the best steak you ever stabbed with a fork. Deal?"

"Thank you, Dusty," Bridget whispered. "We'll see you here at eight then."

In the room, Delores had a number of things going through her mind where Dusty and now Bridget was concerned, but first, she decided they both needed something else to wear other than these old buckskins she had gotten off of Nappy.

"Let's go see what kind of clothes we can buy around here, so we don't have to put these old clothes back on after a nice hot bath. I would like to feel clean for a little while at least."

"We can start at the mercantile store that's across the street." Bridget told her sister. Now she was looking forward to some new clothes.

"Oh my!" Delores exclaimed as they walked from the saloon and realized their wagon was still out front.

As she contemplated what to do with the wagon and team, a young boy walked up to it and started to lead it away.

"Young man," she said in a loud voice to get his attention. "What are you doing taking my wagon?"

"I work at the livery stable and I was told to fetch the wagon and team from in front of the saloon and to bed them down for the night."

"Okay then, just make sure you have them back here no later than nine o'clock in the morning."

"Yes, ma'am. I was already told that."

Interlocking her arm with that of her sister, Delores and Bridget headed across the street to see what they could find for new clothes. The clothes they found had a lot to be desired, but the bath was hot and refreshing. Dusty had been right. The old woman took good care of them. Dusty proved right again with the steaks.

Now back in their room, both ready for bed, Bridget started to say something but her sister stopped her.

"Tomorrow dear, tomorrow. Right now all I want to do is close my eyes and let a good night's sleep refresh these bones. Especially my sore bottom."

Down the hall, Dusty was making ready for bed himself. Lying in the dark, his mind was full of the day's happenings. As enjoyable and unexpected as the evening had turned out, the thought that bothered and troubled him the most was, how easy it had become for him to kill another man.

CHAPTER 4

On the stage coach, Finch and Sam rode in silence. The morning's happenings fresh in their minds.

"Knowing the real identity of the sisters, it was apparent why they would sneak out, but why were they on this stage in the first place?" a question that kept circling round and round in Harry's mind.

The day was already getting hot and the air sticky, but at least the trail had smoothed out some and they were tossed around far less than the day before.

The snorting of the horses and the clippity-clop of their steps were the only sounds filling the morning's air.

"There has to be a reason for those sisters being on this stage and dressed the way they were?" Finch said out loud. His mind just couldn't get past that question.

"That's it!" Finch uttered.

"What's it?" Sam started to ask. But before he could get the question all the way out, Finch had his head out the stages window and hollered up to the driver to stop the stage.

The driver wouldn't normally stop at a passenger's request, but he had been introduced to Finch when he first boarded the stage and thought he was along to guard the money he was transporting.

The driver stopped the stage and both Finch and Sam got out and waited for the driver to step down.

"You see something I didn't?" the driver asked, looking around with one hand on his six-shooter in readiness for trouble.

The stage driver's actions confirmed to Finch what he had come to believe in the past few minutes.

"What are you hauling that I should know about?" Finch asked the driver.

The driver, bewildered by Finch's question didn't know what to answer.

"What are you hauling?" Finch repeated. "Are you hauling a strongbox?"

"You know I'm hauling a strongbox! Why else would you be on board but to protect it?"

"No. I didn't know you were hauling." The look he shot Sam didn't need a question attached to it, but he asked it anyways. "You knew?"

The slight nod of Sam's head indicated that he did know.

The driver continued. "When me and Butch saw those two women get on the stage and right before that being introduced to you, we figured you were on their trail. They are those two women who have been holding up stage coaches. Right?"

"I think they are," said Sam. "Been trying to catch up with them for some time now and this was as close as I've ever come."

Knowing that the driver couldn't tell them anything more then what Nappy had, Finch indicated it was time to move on. There was one more overnight stop before they would get to Cripple Creek and that would be Thunder Point.

The information he had been able to compile from some of the agents there working undercover told him that Slade used this place as a sort of hide away when things got too hot or when he was being pursued. He was hoping he just might run into Slade Rawlins there and take him by surprise.

As the stage got under way, Sam and Finch turned to general conversation about their lives and the path Sam had chosen. Still filled with unanswered questions, Finch pursued the one he was most anxious to have answered.

"There's more to your story than you're letting on," Finch finally said. "You could have easily followed those two sisters and captured them in no time either on the trail or in Eastman where you know they would have to put up for the night."

Finch considered himself somewhat of an expert at extracting information from a suspect, especially from someone who is hiding something or has knowledge of something. The gnawing feeling in the pit of his stomach told him he was correct in both cases where Sam was concerned, but those questions and answers would have to wait to get answered as a new scene started to open up starting with a loud, "whoa" from the driver, followed by two thunderous explosions that Finch recognized as coming from a Colt Peacemaker.

From inside the stage Sam whispered, "I got a lone highwayman on my side, Finch."

"Same here," replied Finch. His Colt already out, cocked and ready for action.

From somewhere on his person, Finch saw that Sam had pulled-up a Colt also. The shiny, chrome plated barrel giving off a quick flash of reflected sunlight that no doubt was also seen by the robber.

Finch was right. The stage robber had caught the flash of light, but before he could act on it, he heard as well as saw the cloud of smoke coming off the end of it. The last thing his eyes would witness on this green earth was an ounce of lead entering the center of his chest, exploding his heart into a million pieces. He felt no pain as he tumbled to the ground. His eyes, black with death, didn't see the ground his bandana-covered face landed on.

Finch's Colt proved just as deadly, although his split second hesitation had allowed the stage robber to get a shot off. A shot that could have killed him, or his partner, or in this case, driver, shotgun, or Sam. The two pistol blasts inside the stage temporarily deafened them.

As the acid smell of discharged gunpowder reached their nostrils, each opened up the stages doors and exited the stage. Colt in one hand, the other over an ear. The stage driver and shotgun were hastily scanning the area surrounding the stage, aware that there could be more robbers. Finch and Sam did the same, but it would appear these two were the only ones. Walking over to the robber he had shot, Sam bent down and removed the bandana that covered his face.

"You're just a kid!" the other three heard him utter.

"This one's just a boy," he hollered over at Finch, who, himself had just removed the mask the robber he had shot wore.

Looking at the soft complexion face, free of any hair stubble, Finch repeated Sam's words. "So is mine."

Of the many lives Finch had taken in his career as a US Marshal, the youngster laying in a heap, dead on the ground at his feet looked to be the youngest he had ever killed.

Walking over to where Sam knelt beside the other dead robber, it was quite apparent to Finch they were related, most likely brothers.

"What do you suppose made them do such a fool thing?" questioned Sam.

Shaking his head, Finch responded to Sam's question

"I don't rightly know, but unless these two came from money, I'd say those four-hundred dollar, custom made boots, tells me it wasn't their first rodeo."

"We best get going if we are to make Thunder Point while there is still daylight," the driver said, confident there were no other robbers lurking around.

Looking over at the big gray mare, Finch said. "Looks like you'll be riding with a dead man, Sam. I have a horse that needs a rider and my backside tells me it can't take another mile of being tossed around in that box."

"Not so fast," uttered Sam. "Help me load my body in the coach will ya? Appears I have a vacant saddle to."

As soon as the bodies were loaded, the stage was under way, except this time at a faster pace.

The dust being kicked up, forced Finch and Sam to fall back to where the stage was just in sight, even then there was still some dust that lingered in the hot, humid air. The sun was just about set when they rode into Thunder Point.

The coach went along to the livery stable, while Finch and Sam tied up in front of the building that had a hanging sign that read 'Sheriff.'

Just as they were to step onto the boardwalk, the door to the sheriff's office opened and a short, chunky fella wearing a big bushy mustache and a silver star pinned to his vest stepped out.

A loud ruckus noise coming from the only saloon in Thunder Point caught the immediate attention of the sheriff, who pulled the door closed with haste and hightailed it over to the saloon without even acknowledging the presence of Finch and Sam.

Before he reached the saloon, a cowboy came flying out through the bat wing doors of the saloon, arms and legs flailing the air and landing with a loud thud in a cloud of dust in the street.

As the three looked on, this cowboy foolishly went for his shooter which had come out of its holster and laid in the dirt next to him. As they watched, a larger than life figure appeared standing between the pushed-opened bat wings. In the next instant, the roar from his quickly drawn six-guns filled the night's air and two well aimed rounds of hot lead entered the cowboy's chest. In the next moment, both Finch and Sam heard a loud, "Slade," yelled from the sheriff's mouth, then watched as the events unwrapped before them in slow motion, or so they seemed. Without a blink from his eye, Slade turned and unloaded another two rounds from his still smoking six-guns into the sheriff who dropped dead in his tracks.

Before either Finch or Sam could react, both were staring down the smoking barrels of Slade's feared and deadly six-guns. Finch had never been in a predicament like this before, either on the job or off in his whole lifetime. He had never been faced with death so up and close as right now, where his next decision would determine his future.

Finch knew there was no chance of out-gunning two already aimed Colts, which were still smoking from the death of two others in the hands of such a fearless killer. So when he heard Slade's voice ask the question, his pure will to survive took over.

"Live or join them. Choice is yours, boys!" was all that Finch heard.

"Not our fight, friend," Finch uttered, lowering his hands till they dangled at his side. Sam doing the same.

"Smart," he told them. As he continued pointing his guns in their direction, Slade made his way to a big black stallion tied up next to the saloon.

Holstering one of his guns, Slade stepped up into the saddle while keeping his other trained at the two. Slowly coaching a slow walk from his ride, Slade tipped the rim of his Stetson with his gun barrel, placed two rounds of lead at their feet and galloped off into the night's air and disappeared, before the dust caused by the two shots at their feet settled.

As quickly has it had begun, the happenings that had just taken place were over. People had already stepped out and were at the side of the dead sheriff and cowboy.

"You two are some lucky partners," Finch heard someone say. "Slade don't usually stop when there is someone before him going for their pistols like you two were. No sir. Not at all. I'd count yourselves.......Well I don't know what to count yourselves. Some kinda blessed, I'd guess."

"Does anyone know who this cowboy is?" asked Finch.

"Never seen him before," was the only answer he received. "But that there was sheriff Tuttle. Wife passed just this spring. No kin I know of," looking at Finch, then in the direction Slade had ridden out in, remarked. "Someone needs to put an end to his killin'. He rides in here like king poop, guns down anyone who so much as flinches around him. Planted three fellas in Boot Hill this past year," nodding at the cowboy lying dead at their feet, uttered, "he makes four."

"Just what I plan on doing," Finch heard Sam reply, as he stepped around the dead cowboy and walked into the saloon.

Finch made his way over to the sheriff's office. Entering, he noticed how cold it felt, even though it was still hot outside. Death had a way of making one's surroundings feel like that, he surmised. It was a one room office with a jail cell against the back wall, which was empty, its door open and the key hanging from a peg in the wall behind the sheriff's desk. Pot-belly stove in the corner was cold and so was the half a pot of coffee which sat on top of it. The office was clean and orderly. Finch saw a small pile of papers on the desk and went over to it and picked them up.

One piece of paper was a note that simply read, 'Your boots are fixed and ready.' The other two were telegrams. One concerned the two dead coach robbers that he and Sam had killed, who were taking their last ride to the undertakers before joining the many others in Boot Hill. Seems they were brothers and each had a small bounty of five hundred dollars on their heads.

"I'll be sure to tell Sam about that," he said out loud. "That will make him happy."

Next telegram was from the sheriff of Cripple Creek warning him that Slade was headed in his direction. That one message was troubling for Finch and the questions came rushing up in his brain, as always, when it was fed information. Before Finch could start to sort out the many questions that surfaced, a woman's voice was heard coming from the open door which he hadn't closed.

Turning to face the voice, Finch was confronted by a beautiful woman to be in her mid-twenties, who, by her dress was a saloon girl, dancer or both.

"I'm Amanda," she said, offering up her hand.

Quickly removing his hat, Finch took her extended hand in his and introduced himself.

"I'm Finch, Harry Finch, ma'am," he blurted out, his tongue getting all tied up in his mouth. "Most just call me Finch."

Smiling at his awkwardness, but knowing the effect she had on men who met her for the first time she said his name. "Harry Finch," looking into his eyes she repeated his name then decided and told him, "I like Harry."

"Looks like I'm about finished up here. Would you like to get some supper with me?"

It was a brave move on his part and one he had never taken until now, but there was something about the effect this woman had on him he couldn't understand.

"I'd love to have supper with you Harry, but under one condition," she said, interlocking her arm in his and leading him out the door. "You let me cook it."

The fried chicken was the juiciest that Harry had sank his teeth into in a long time, not to mention the green beans, mashed potatoes and golden brown biscuits smothered in butter and honey.

When Harry thought he couldn't eat another bite without exploding, Amanda sat a dish of apple cobbler in front of him and poured a fresh steaming cup of black coffee.

Sliding the cobbler away, Harry told her. "I'm so full I don't believe I could enjoy that cobbler worthy of what it smells like," he told her. "Let's take our coffee and go sit on that swing on the front porch."

"I'd like that," she said in a soft tender voice, and then leaned in and gave him a soft, inviting kiss on the lips.

Many kisses followed as they sat sipping their coffee and learning more and more about each other. Amanda had arrived in Thunder Point less than a year ago on her way to Cripple Creek, where she was to be employed by a Doctor Benson, when what she regards as fate stepped in.

"When I arrived here, sheriff Tuttle's wife was near death. When he learned I was a nurse, he asked if I would look in on her which I did of course."

Here, Harry picked up sadness in her voice.

A simple rose thorn," she said. Can you imagine that, Harry? Infection from a rose thorn killed that woman."

Harry gave Amanda the comfort she desired for that moment. Soon, she continued her story.

"I learned that the town had been without a doctor for the past year. Several of the town's people had died from simple causes, not to mention the shape several of the working girls were in, due to drunken cowboys needing to take their frustrations of not being able to perform out on them. I decided to stay."

"I'm glad you did," murmured Harry through their joined lips.

Separating so he could catch his breath and composure, Harry whispered in her ear.

"I'm ready for some of that cobbler now."

Feeling Harry's hot breath on her neck and knowing the feelings running through her body were the same he was feeling, she pulled herself away. The sparkle she saw in his eyes and the boyish look on his face told her all she needed to know right then.

The past year of nursing everyone's wounds and not taking time for herself was about to come to an end. This man, this Harry Finch, had set in motion feelings she hadn't felt in a very long time.

"I hope you're ready for more than cobbler!" she exclaimed, pulling him to his feet and leading him back inside.

CHAPTER 5

It wasn't the bright slivers of morning sunlight coming in through the open window that woke Finch up. Nor was it the sweet smell of lavender. It was the loud screeching, "Errt-uhh-err-uh-errrrrrr?" coming from the old cock rooster telling everyone that dawn had arrived and it was time to get-up and greet a new day.

As Harry started to wake-up he was aware of the weight on his right shoulder. Turning his head in that direction, his lips turned upward in a smile, as he remembered where and who he was with and the happenings from the previous evening.

She's as beautiful sleeping as when she's awake, Harry's eyes told him. I don't even know who you are, and yet, here I am, sharing your bed. These feelings Finch had at that moment were ones he had felt once before, early on in his career.

It was love at first sight also, but he was building his career and had been one hundred percent honest with her. He told her of the dangers, of the weeks and maybe months he might be away on an assignment. The cold dinners she would fix, waiting for him on the table as he worked late.

Finch had told her everything. He had seen it all firsthand being the son of a US Marshal. He had quietly stayed in his room and listened once again to his mom and dad argue concerning his dad's work and the hours not spent at home, until she had enough and one day, she was gone. So, Finch had lived his life not ever thinking of a lasting relationship. Never mind marriage and kids.

Amanda had started to stir.

First, he felt the arm draped across his chest, tighten to draw him in even closer to the warm body snuggled against his. Then, one eye opened and then the other, blinking to get the sleep from them. The rich, sparkling hazel green of her eyes came alive with the bands of sunlight that fell across her face, slowly turning upward to gaze upon his face. Harry could almost make out his reflection in them.

The sweet, red lips turning upward in a smile that instantly had a memorizing effect on him. There was no denying it, Finch was in love with this woman he held in his arms. Her smile, her voice, her body, her smell, all invaded his senses together, not to mention she was also a fantastic cook.

Now they're looking into each other's eyes. Finch felt like he had known her all his life. Finch was just about to taste her lips for the thousandth time when a sharp knock was heard startling them both.

Finch looked on as Amanda rose and wrapped her naked body with a robe she removed from the hook on the back of the bedroom door. Even in the bedroom, everything had its place, he thought as he continued watching her. Finch listened as she called out through the door, asking who was there.

"Sam, ma'am," came the reply. "If Harry Finch is in there with you, would you have him come to the door? It's very important."

"He is here," she informed him. "I'll get him. I'm about to make some coffee and breakfast if you'd like to join us."

"Thanks for the offer, ma'am. I really need to just have a word with Harry, and I'll be on my way."

"Suit yourself," she replied. "Harry's right here."

"Morning, Harry," Sam said. "Sorry to bother you, but…"

"But what, Sam? What is so important that you would track me down and come knocking on a stranger's door at dawn?" Harry was visibly upset by Sam's being there.

"I need to know what your plans are." The excitement in his voice told Finch something was up. And Sam giving recognition to the killer Slade, who they had encountered yesterday, told him this probably had something to do with this moment.

"Is your business in Cripple Creek have anything to do with Slade?" he questioned. "Cause if it does, I need to talk seriously to you about him."

Not knowing if he was making the right decision in telling him that he was, Finch turned to Amanda and asked her to make some fresh coffee. Without questioning him, she nodded her head and headed for the kitchen, while Harry pushed open the screen door and invited Sam in.

Once inside, Harry led Sam into the parlor where they both took seats. Harry and Sam sat in silence gazing at each other. This is how Amanda found them upon entering with two steaming cups of coffee and a small dish of cakes, which she sat on the coffee table separating the two.

"You two enjoy. I'm going to leave you two, but if there is anything else you need, just call." Walking out of the room, she turned and said, "The pot is on the stove, help yourselves to more coffee."

The next sound heard, was the closing of her bedroom door.

"I'm going to Cripple Creek to arrest and bring to justice Slade," Harry said, breaking the silence, then reaching for the cup of coffee that had been placed before him, not taking his eyes off of Sam.

Taking a sip of coffee, Harry waited for Sam's reaction, while at the same time, noting the rich flavor of the hot coffee that filled his mouth.

"What is your interest in Slade?" Harry asked. Turning the question around and back to him.

Sam reached into his vest pocket and extracted a folded up piece of paper which he unfolded before handing it to Harry.

"That's the newest poster on him," Sam spoke. "I would reckon it will be considerably more with the cold bloody murder of the sheriff we witnessed yesterday."

"Twenty-five thousand dollars reward," Finch read aloud. "Dead or alive," he continued.

"I know all this!" Finch exclaimed, handing the wanted poster back to Sam and waiting for more information.

"I want that bounty, Finch," Sam blurted out, taking the poster and folding it back up and returning it to his breast pocket.

"You can't claim it being a Marshal an all, but I can. And I will, providing you give me the opportunity to do so."

"By your statement, you're asking me to let you claim that bounty? Is that what I'm hearing?" asked Finch.

"What you're hearing here, is me asking that you delay your leaving here for a couple of days," he answered. "I've been waiting for this kind of payday for a while now, Harry," he said, excitement showing in his voice.

"I was trailing those two sisters 'cause I heard they were going to meet up with him. Word got out one of them was raped a while back and they were looking to hire him to kill the man responsible.”

“Why didn’t they have him arrested and stand trial?” Harry asked, taking a sip of his coffee.

“They did!” exclaimed Sam. “The jury found him innocent because he was a prominent figure in town. He hired the best lawyers he could and before the trial was over, they had her looking like a common street whore.”

Sam stood up and walked to the door.

“Normally, I wouldn’t be bothered by any of this, but when I heard they were looking to find Slade and hire him, I knew this might be the break I was looking for in finding him myself.”

Turning back to face Finch, Sam repeated his request.

“Two days, Harry. That’s all I’m asking for. Two days.”

“Any chance of you giving up this life and coming back to the Agency?” Harry knew the answer, but needed to be sure.

“They’d take you back, I’m sure,” he said. And he would probably be right in saying that.

“No desire, Finch!” he said with a smirk on his face

“But Sam! You were well liked, except near the end,” Finch told him. “You were good at your job.”

"No desire." This time, the smirk was gone and replaced by a drop-the-subject look.

Harry knew when to quit with the questions and this was one of those times.

"Okay! Subject is dropped," Finch said in a low voice, hoping his softened the voice would quiet Sam down. The last thing Harry wanted was any kind of confrontation with Sam.

"I'll ask one more time, Harry. Give me two days head start. If when I get to Cripple Creek, Slade is gone, I'll leave word for you as to the direction I'll be traveling."

"And if he's there?" Finch asked.

"Well, if I find him there, he will probably be waiting for his place in Boot Hill by the time you arrive. But I'll make certain they wait to bury him until you get there and sign off on that reward money," hoping to convince Finch to give him what he's asking for, he added, "I'd be willing to share a small portion of that reward money with you, Harry," Sam offered, knowing perfectly well that Finch wouldn't take any money.

"I want him alive, Sam," said Finch. "If you will give me your word that you will do everything to try to make that possible, well then, I will give you those two days."

Sam couldn't have been more surprised by Harry agreeing to give him what he had asked for and the look on his face showed that.

"The reward money is the same alive or dead," Sam stated. "I won't have to transport or feed him other than to the jail house to lock him up till you arrive. So, if I can take him alive I will, but no promises that he will co-operate."

"You have two days," said Harry, not quite knowing why he was agreeing to Sam's request, but decided he would go against his gut feeling. "Best be riding."

Nothing more was said between the two. Sam gave a simple nod of thanks, turned and was gone.

As Finch watched him ride off, he knew that he had probably signed off on the death of Slade. Sam's own words told him that, but he was hoping that, given the situation at hand, Sam might take him alive. After all, he had agreed to at least try. Either outcome, Finch decided then and there he wouldn't compromise his character ever again.

Amanda came back into the room having heard Sam ride off. Even though they hadn't known each other for long, she sensed what Finch was feeling at that moment and went to his side and placed her hand on his shoulder.

After a few minutes, Harry gave out a loud sigh and exclaimed, "I'm famished! Let's go get something to eat."

Wrapping his arms around her waist, Harry looked into her eyes and said to her, "Then I want to spend the day getting to know you."

"I'd like that same thing," she told him, placing a tender yet passionate kiss on his lips.

After breakfast, Amanda and Harry rode out of town. Harry was going to rent a carriage, but Amanda told him she wanted to ride because there was a special place she wanted to take him that a carriage couldn't reach. She wouldn't even let Harry saddle a horse for her, but did it herself as if she wanted to prove to him she just wasn't a warm body to occupy his bed at night, but also a woman who was capable of taking care of herself.

Finch had noticed the difference in Amanda as they saddled up. Gone were her frilly clothes, replaced now by stylish pants, form fitting, deep red, balloon sleeved blouse, to match her ruby red lips, well-worn boots and topped off by a snow white Stetson with a hat band made up of silver Conchos and turquoise stones.

The morning rays of sunlight seemed to shimmer off her golden blond hair. Finch stood looking at her and the love he felt earlier was magnified a hundred fold. He noticed she slung a beautifully tooled set of saddle bags over the hindquarters of her mare and wondered what she had in them.

Stepping up into the saddle, she turned and with a big grin on her face asked, "Ready cowboy?"

Moments later she dug her heels into the mare's sides and bolted off like a shot, leaving Harry, who hadn't mounted up yet, standing in a cloud of dust watching her gallop away.

"Wait for me," Harry bellowed out after her.

Grabbing the saddle horn with his left hand, Harry flung himself up onto the saddle and took off after her. Glancing back over her shoulder, Amanda saw that Harry was up in the saddle and was galloping in her direction. Pulling back on their reins, Amanda slowed her mount down allowing Harry time to catch up to her.

"Hey, little lady! Where did you learn to ride like that?" asked Harry, pulling up next to her.

"Well, when you have four older brothers, you learn to do the same stuff they like or get left behind," she told him.

"You have four brothers?" Finch questioned.

"Yup," she answered. "We were a close knit family and learned to rely on each other, and me being the only sister, all were very protective of me."

Harry was just about to ask another question, but before he could, Amanda continued.

"We're almost to the spot I wanted to take you so let's ride on in silence and enjoy the ride. We have a beautiful morning and there will be plenty of time to ask each other questions, as the day lingers on."

A click click of her tongue encouraged her mount into a brisk trot. Harry got the hint and prodded his mount into a similar trot keeping a little distance between them.

Leaving the main trail, Amanda led them to an area where she reined to a stop and dismounted. Taking her saddlebag and bedroll she stood and waited for Harry. She was glad Harry had listened to her and stopped asking questions. The few times when she had the opportunity to go for a ride, she did so alone and liked to be surrounded by silence.

Harry pulled up beside her and dismounted. He had granted Amanda her wish for silence, and in doing so, his brain went into overload and he was ready to ask the question, so he could get to know her better. Handing Harry, the bedroll, she motioned for him to follow her.

After walking a hundred yards or so, they stood before a glistening pool of water that was surrounded by a large rock formation. The only thing that could have improved the setting better would have been a waterfall. There was no waterfall, but a large creek flowing into the pool.

Amanda took her bedroll back from Harry and spread it out on the pools bank close to the water's edge.

"Time to sit," she indicated to Harry.

Opening the saddle bag, she took out a mason jar which was filled with coffee and sat it between them.

Next, a couple of tin cups, one of which she handed to Harry.

"So tell me what you want to know about me?" she said with a smile on her face. "I will tell you anything you want to know."

The next hour or so was filled with conversation. First one, then the other, would ask a question and the other would answer. Once the coffee was gone, Amanda stood up and reached for her saddle bag.

"Close your eyes," she said. "And no peeking. You are about to witness something no one before you has ever witnessed."

Closing his eyes, Harry's mind once again went into high gear wondering what it could be. He didn't have to wait long before he heard her tell him.

"Okay, you can open them now," she said, having moved so she stood right in front of him.

Harry was caught off guard, there before him stood Amanda sporting a matched pair of 45's beautifully displayed in what had to be the most beautiful set of holsters he had ever laid his eyes on. Both were tied off low on her thighs, such as a professional gunslinger would wear them.

"Ever seen a pair of these on a woman before?" she asked Harry, who stood there before her wearing a surprised look on his face.

"Nope!" he exclaimed. "But there again, I have never met anyone quite like you before."

"Do you approve of a woman wearing side arms just like a man would?" she questioned.

"You any good with those?" he asked, ignoring her question.

Without speaking, Amanda turned from him. With speed so quick his vision was blurred, Amanda drew one of her pistols and fanned off six shots so fast, the barrel blast sounded as one.

Harry stood there with a dropped chin and a pure look of disbelief on his face, never had he witnessed such speed before, never mind coming from a woman.

"Well, Marshal," she said after a few passing moments. "What's your verdict?

As she spoke, she was busy emptying the spent shells from the pistols chambers and replacing them with fresh ones. As he watched, she bent down and picked up the used cartridges and drop them into the saddle bag.

"That's not normal behavior," Harry told himself. "That's a learned habit for survival, if you were any kind of lawman or gunfighter!

"First thing you're taught in Marshal school is to reload your firearm the second you are done firing it, whether you fired one chamber or many, you reload.

There's a lot more to this woman that I have to know about."

Finch's heart pounded in his chest and his ears rang from the loud blasts from Amanda's 45.

"I'm impressed," he told her. The grin on his face went from ear to ear. "I'm impressed."

CHAPTER 6

Sam rode the trail to Cripple Creek as fast as his ride would allow. If he knew what lay ahead, he might have been a little less hasty, but dollar signs in his head propelled him on. After all, a twenty-five-thousand-dollar bounty would be the largest sum of money he had ever collected and a good share of it he had already spent.

As Sam rode on, he had a feeling he was being dogged but had seen no one, even his mount was a little jittery, a good indication he had picked up a scent in the air or his ears had heard the sounds of another horse or that of a bobcat, bear, or mountain lion, all of which were a threat. "If I'm being followed, it sure would be difficult to see anyone. The thickets and boulders that lined the trail would offer much cover for someone or something planning an ambush," Sam thought to himself.

As he rode on, he listened for any sounds that would indicate there was someone following him but he heard none. The air was quiet except for the clop, clop sounds of his horse's footsteps on the hard, dry trail and the creaking sounds coming from his saddle.

The trail opened into a large clearing, which offered no cover so that anyone following him would be exposed. Reaching the other side of the clearing, Sam turned so he could watch the trail. Several minutes passed and no other person rode into view.

Now convinced he wasn't being followed, Sam kicked his ride into a trot. Once again his thoughts were on Cripple Creek and the hopes he would find Slade there.

Cripple Creek was nothing like Sam had imagined it to be. For one, it was a lot bigger with lots and lots of brightly painted buildings sporting signs telling a passerby what to expect inside. Tying up in front of a building with a sign that read, 'Cripple Creek Hotel and Gambling Emporium,' Sam stood and gazed up and down the main street which was still alive with shoppers.

The clattering of a roulette wheel was the first sound Sam heard even before he pushed open the bat wing doors and stepped inside.

"Gosh! I've missed that sound," he thought as he stepped inside. His eyes automatically drawn to that sound and that of a loud voice calling out, "Twenty-three red." All eyes immediately went to the table to see if there were any chips on twenty-three red and to who might be a winner. The sequenced red and black numbers on the table's layout was covered in chips. The only thing that covered twenty-three red was a piece of gold that appeared to be a gold tooth.

As everyone around the table voiced their, "ohhhhhhhs," the Groupier placed a marker next to the gold tooth and proceeded to rake off all the chips that were on the losing numbers. Sam's eyes scanned everyone's faces looking for the person who bore the nickname, "The Tooth Fairy."

Little was known concerning the person who had become known as "The Tooth Fairy" other than he had a price on his head and if you sported a gold tooth and crossed paths with him, your life span was surely going to be shortened or at least that of your gold tooth.

The price on "The Tooth Fairy's" head was only five hundred dollars. He had never killed any of his victims, only hitting them on the head knocking them out then extracting the gold tooth leaving them with a toothless smile. Sam watched as several chips and the gold tooth were slid across the layout to the only winner. Sam couldn't have been more surprised at who "The Tooth Fairy" was.

Sitting at the table behind the pile of chips that was just pushed to him was a little, well dressed, balding man looking to be in his mid to late forties.

Sam watched as he picked up the gold tooth, taking a small pouch from his breast pocket dropped it in then returned it back to his pocket, picked his winnings up and left the table and walked to the bar where he placed the chips on the bar top and traded them in for cash money.

Sam was tempted right then and there to apprehend "The Tooth-Fairy" but that would have given him away and he had a much bigger fish to catch, so he just watched as he counted the cash money that was exchanged for his chips. Satisfied with the exchange, he pocketed his winnings and turned to leave the bar, but before he could a loud voice was heard.

"Riker!" This was the name heard above all the noise in the gambling house and one that made "The Tooth Fairy" stop and turn in its direction. Sam noticed a cowboy, standing up by one of the tables, had drawn his pistol. As if in slow motion, Sam saw several men dive out of its path just as a loud "Boooom" was heard followed by a gray cloud of smoke.

Sam noticed the shear look of horror on "The Tooth Fairy's" face, as the ounce of lead drilled into his chest and exited out his back, spurting blood and flesh matter all over the bar-top. Hands went up to clutch his chest where the bullet had entered, as legs buckled at the knees. The place had become deadly quiet and the "thuuuud" of the now dead "Tooth-Fairy" could be heard hitting the floor.

As quick as the action had begun, it also ended. Over-turned chairs were up-righted and once again filled with a person's body. The clattering of the roulette wheel, followed by, "place your bets," signaled once again, business as usual. Sam watched as the cowboy who had done the killing, approach the body, crouched down and took the small pouch containing the gold teeth from his breast pocket. Standing, his gaze meet Sam's.

Slowly his lips turned up in an open-mouth grin, exposing two blank spaces where Sam guessed two gold teeth once occupied.

Two men approached the dead body and simply reached down and grabbed a hold of a foot and dragged him out the door and down the street to the undertaker. "Riker," "The Tooth Fairy," or whoever he was, was about to have his rendezvous with Boot Hill.

Sam had thought of speaking with the town's marshal about maybe laying claims to the bounty offered, but he was out of town, and besides, he didn't want to bring attention to himself. Sam had spent almost no time in the west, so he wasn't too worried about being called out as a bounty hunter.

As the afternoon's sky took on the many brilliant shades of reds, yellows, blues and pinks, Sam was reminded that this was the end of the two days head start Finch had promised him. Tomorrow, Harry would be saddled up and headed in his direction.

"No sign of Slade," he thought as he continued watching the two drag the body down the street. A door being slammed closed, caught his attention and he turned in its direction.

"Just a shop keeper locking up for the night," the small voice whispered in his head. The sounds of a barking dog turned Sam's head to look in its direction. Doing so he saw two men on horseback lazily entering town. Too far away to recognize either figure, Sam stepped backwards into the shadow offered by the overhung second story porch of the hotel, so that he could observe the two men without being noticed.

Still unnoticed as he stood in the shadows, the two men reined up in front of the hotel and dismounted. Neither one spoke as they looped their horse's reins over the hitching post and stepped up onto the boardwalk and through the bat-wing doors of the hotel/saloon.

"Slade!" Sam's mind cried out recognizing one of the figures. "But, who's the other one?"

Sam didn't recognize him although he kinda remembered hearing about a black man wanted for some murders down south a year or two back.

"What was his name?" Sam repeated over and over again in his mind. Drawing a blank, Sam was sure someone should be able to answer that question.

Now that Sam knew "Slade" was in town and where he was, it should be easy to observe him without being noticed.

"Although he wouldn't know me as a bounty hunter, he might remember me from our earlier encounter." This was one of many thoughts going through his mind at this time along with knowing he now had just two days before Finch rode into town to arrest "Slade."

The sudden, loud crack of thunder startled Sam. He knew he needed to get somewhere inside in a hurry or else he was going to get drenched. Sam untied his horse and headed to the livery stable to board him.

"Do you know a fella who goes by the name "Slade?" he asked the livery keep.

"Who wants to know?" came his reply.

Before Sam could answer, the livery keep said, "Never mind. Don't care who you are, learned a long time ago not to question a stranger's request, especially one who's either a law-dog or a bounty hunter. Don't see no star, so I figure you're the latter one, but the answers come with a price."

Another crack of thunder followed by a bolt of lightning brought snorting and nickering from the many horses bedded down inside. Sam took a five-dollar gold piece from his vest and indicated that's what he was going to pay for his answers. With a slight head nod from the livery keep, Sam extended his hand and dropped the coin in his hand.

"Ya, I know "Slade," he told Sam. "Rode into town a few minutes ago."

"You saw him then?" Sam was hoping now he could also tell him who the other man was.

"Of course I saw him. Rode in with Brother Baker."

Sam continued on with his questions not believing his good luck already finding someone who knew who this other man was with "Slade."

"Brother Baker? Don't know the name," Said Sam.

"Most folks around here know him by "Reverend," Sam was told. "He's a gunslinger and someone you don't want to mess with."

"Never heard of him," Sam said. Curious now as to why he hadn't heard the name before.

"You might know him by his other name, "Crow!"

At the mention of that name, Sam's head turned up, so did his eye brows.

"Crow," he repeated the name. "You sure?"

"Of course I'm sure. Only black gunslinger around."

Well now, Sam had a name and one he recalled now that he had been reminded of it.

A low rumbling sound was heard off in the distance and increased in volume until it exploded into a thunderbolt that shook the livery stable and spooked the horses half to death. Along with it came a downpour of rain that had the street flooded over in a matter of minutes.

"Won't last long," Sam was told. "Never does. Just long enough to flood the streets and turn them into muddy messes."

"Do you have anyone who can go over to the hotel and rent me a room?" He asked.

An ear piercing whistle brought a young boy out from one of the rear stalls. Giving the boy the price of a room plus a couple extra pennies, Sam watched as he ran out into the rain and disappeared into the night. Sam instructed him to make sure he had an outside accessible room. He was also to look around to see what Slade and the Reverend were doing.

While waiting for the boy to return, Sam found out the livery keeper was Joe Riley and that Slade had a ranch just outside of town. It was a horse ranch and he had about seven hired hands working there. Joe didn't know if they were all gunmen or not, but was sure at least two were as they usually came into town with Slade and wore twin draw holsters. This was the first he had seen the Reverend in several months.

"When he comes to town, he and his men mind their own business. They pay their bills and don't look for trouble. He usually finds out rather quickly if there are any new folk in town."

"What's the chances he knows about me?" Sam asked.

"We'll know when the boy returns," Joe told him.

Ten minutes passed before a soaking wet boy came running into the livery. Sam learned that his presence was known, although, no one knew who he was.

"I probably wouldn't sleep to soundly tonight." Sam was told. "Expect a midnight visit from either him or a couple of his men," Joe told Sam. "I don't know what your business is here Sam, but if you're a law dog or a low snake bounty hunter, I'd be riding out of town. Both have tried to come here and take him down and now they're pushing up daisies. Joe waited till the next thunderbolt had ended before continuing.

"In the past when Reverend had come to town, the bounty hunter known as Two-tone, because a birth defect had created a dark patch over half his face had arrived and made it known he was looking for Slade and wasn't about to leave till he had found him."

Sam was enjoying the story when a bolt of lightning lite up the sky, exposing the figure of someone headed in their direction.

"Someone's coming," Sam said scurrying to get out of sight.

Joe motioned for him to lay down. Once he did, a canvas tarp was thrown over him and over that, Sam figured some loose hay.

"Evening, Joe."

"Well! Gosh darn, if it isn't Walt. What brings you out on a night like this?" Sam heard Joe ask.

"Slade heard there was a stranger in town and figured if there was he would have been boarding his ride with you. Have you seen this stranger, Joe?"

Walt was one of Slade's right hand men and was believed to be a gunman, so Joe knew he had better be careful and chose his words careful.

"A stranger did ride in today and I have his horse right over there."

Walt looked in the direction Joe nodded, and saw the large Bay.

"Told me his name was Sam and was passing through until the storm hit, then he decided to spend the night. Thought he was over at the hotel."

"Only new guy registered at the hotel is a Sam Colter and was told that your stable boy registered him."

Joe knew right away that he was in deep horse crap and his life was on the line as well as the boys. Another thunder clap and lighting bolt lit up the stable, and with it, Joe saw Walt reach up and clutch his chest before his knees gave way and he fell face down on the hard packed floor. As he fell, the acidy odor of gunpowder reached Joe's nose and his eyes were diverted from Walt's lifeless body to that of Sam's coming up out of the hay that had been covering him.

"Oh my, oh my! What have you done?" Sam heard the frantic voice of Joe calling out. He knew that time was short before others would be coming looking for Walt who laid dead on the floor.

Joe's life as he knew it would be over shortly and Sam knew that. He needed a plan and needed one right now.

Sam's thoughts raced to the incoming Harry and all of a sudden his ex-marshal's mind took over and a plan quickly formed.

"Joe. You and the boy have to get out of here and so do I. We don't have much time to do it. Go to a place where you feel will be safe for you and the boy. I don't think anyone will try to find you. They will be looking for me. Now git out of here, while you can under cover of this storm."

Sam watched them ride out, before he saddled up. He had a good mind to ride back the way he came in hopes of meeting Marshal Finch and together they can work up a plan to get Slade and his small band of hired guns.

Sam also knew Harry's life depended on him intercepting him on the trail. He would be cut down as soon as he entered town, if his presence was known. Sam looped a rope around one of Walt's legs. He would drag him out of town and do his best to hide his body. Sam left the same way Joe had. He would have to ride all night in the dark and the rain, if he had any hope at all of crossing Harry's path.

The rain felt like shot from a shotgun as it hit his face and, soaking through his clothes, soon had him shivering in the night's cooler temperature. He was hoping he was riding in the right direction to intercept Harry.

Little did Sam know just what twist and turns lay ahead.

CHAPTER 7

The trail ride for Harry brought back some fond memories, as well as not so fond ones. He enjoyed being alone on the open trail, listening to the birds and the creaking of the saddle, the ever constant clop, clop of his horse's footsteps, and sleeping out under a shimmering blanket of stars.

Stopping alongside a creek, Harry dismounted and led his horse to the cool water to get a drink. Duke and Harry had been together a long time. The bond between the two, only someone who spent a good portion of his life in the saddle could understand.

"How long has it been now, Duke?" Harry asked out loud, never once stopping to think how ridiculous it might sound to someone else, talking to a horse!

Harry just smiled as Duke raised his head at the sound of his name and swished his tail and gave off a short snort in hearing his name. Harry had often wondered if the bond between husband and wife felt anything like that between horse and rider and, until Amanda, he could only guess the answer. But now he knew. Although similar, they were different.

When it came to Duke, Harry had a great respect for Duke but, "Do I love him?"

Harry thought on that question for a moment and without thinking said out loud, "No."

Duke suddenly raised his head, ears pointing skywards and pawed the earth.

"What is it boy?" came a whispered response to Duke, acknowledging that someone or something was approaching. From around the bend in the trail to Harry's amazement, an Indian squaw appeared followed by two young ones. Seeing him, she stopped and turned to go back wanting to avoid any confrontation. It was then Harry noticed, strapped to her back was a beautifully decorated cradleboard holding an infant.

"It's okay!" he said in a loud enough voice for her to hear, but she and the two little ones disappeared back down the trail from where she had come.

"Well! What do you make of that, Duke?" Harry asked, wishing Duke could talk as it already was becoming lonely out by himself. Duke gave off a low nicker and continued on with his drink.

"Well, old boy, if we're going to make it to Cripple Creek by tomorrow, we best be hitting the trail." Stepping up into the saddle, Harry spurred Duke on.

* * * *

Half-a-day's ride north in the small town of Eastman, Dusty Roberts and the two Avery sisters, Delores and Bridget, were also making their way out of town headed for Cripple Creek. Dusty had also heard about the large bounty on the head of Slade and decided to pursue that option, as to more stage robberies. The two Avery women decided to go with him. Besides, it would be kinda nice riding together after so much time apart, plus Dusty had made them a promise that he would return with them and kill Freeman, knowing they wouldn't be hiring Slade.

It was obvious to Dolores that her sister Bridget and Dusty were still in love and she, for the moment, felt guilty for Dusty leaving at a time when she had needed comfort and the strength that only a man could give. Now, here was a second chance offered her sister at love and she wasn't going to stand between them again. It was Delores who broke the silence.

"It's as plain as the nose on my face; you two still have strong feelings for each other."

The look between the two as she spoke confirmed what she already knew.

"Dusty. You don't have to return and kill Freeman, besides I've been thinking on continuing to California. I've heard about a place called San Francisco and with all the gold out there, maybe I'll find myself a man of my own."

"Buuu." Bridget started to say.

"But nothing. We've been together a long time, neither one ever giving a thought to the day when one of us would fall in love and move on to start a new life. No matter what, when this job is over, I'm headed to

California. If you and Dusty want to tag along fine, but it's time we separate and go it alone for a while."

Listening to her sister, Bridget became fully aware of what she was saying. She had often wonder what would happen if the time came when one fell in love, what would the other do. Now, she knew.

As the three rode on, no one was aware of the two men that followed them until they heard the boom boom made from the muzzle blast from two Colt revolvers. The two sisters spun around to face the two, the third, Dusty, clutched his chest. The last thing his eyes would see on this earth was his blood which spattered the neck of his mount before his eyes blackened over and he toppled to the ground, landing in a cloud of dust. Another victim for the small Boot Hill cemetery of Eastman.

Before either sister could speak, one of the shooters did. Waving his pistol in their faces he began.

"You two ladies have a choice to make and that choice will determine your immediate future. You can continue riding to wherever you are headed and forget these faces, or you can join your yellow-bellied friend lying there on the ground," he looked at his partner, then looked back at them and asked, "What will it be?"

Neither spoke, but instantly spurred their mounts and galloped off in a cloud of dust not slowing down until their mounts gave out from shear exhaustion and simply stopped running and came to an abrupt halt. Delores and

Bridget dismounted and rushed into each other's arms. Grasping each other so tightly, they could feel the pounding of the other's heart. Both burst into tears as the realization of what just happened, along with what could have happened sunk in. The crying soon stopped and the sisters separated but neither spoke.

Bridget was the first to speak.

"Who were those two men?" she asked, breaking out into a quick back and forth step.

"I'd say two men who obviously didn't like Dusty!" Her words were sarcastic and still showed her dislike for him even though a short time ago, they were ones of acceptance.

Delores' words stopped the pacing Bridget and she looked coldly into her sister's face before breaking into uncontrolled sobbing.

"I'm sorry, dear," Delores said. Once again wrapping her arms around her sister.

"Who were those two men?" Bridget repeated once she had regained her senses.

"I don't know," answered her sister, but what I do know is we had best be moving just in case they change their minds and come after us also."

The two sisters had nothing to worry about being followed. The two who had shot and killed Dusty were brothers simply avenging the death of their oldest brother at the hands of Dusty, who when he brought him in strapped across his saddle, had two bullet holes in his back.

"He was trying to escape," was Dusty's story.

The brother's form of justice had come full circle as Dusty lay dead in a heap on the trail with two bullet holes in his back. His body left for the wild animals to devour. A good many thoughts were floating around inside Delores' head, as the two rode on.

"Well, I guess it's back to our original plans of finding this gunman named Slade," said Delores. "So onto Cripple Creek, I guess."

Before he was gunned down, Wade had told the girls they would head to a town named Silver Springs where Slade was also known to visit. It was said he also owned a saloon there and quite a few of the townspeople were beholding to him, so they would have to be careful.

Now that Wade was dead, they would be looking to hire Slade, not gun him down. It was going to be a long ride, and without Wade, they decided to return to Eastman and take the stage to Silver Springs. Before long, the two sisters were once again on a stage being bounced up on down on the hard seats. There were four other passengers on the stage. An old couple and two younger men who were some kind of businessmen by the way they were dressed. Halfway through the trip, Bridget reached across the coach and gave one of the young men a hard slap across the face.

"I'm tired of you staring at my chest so that's just a sampling of what is to come if you continue."

Delores was thinking the same about the little old man who was a little more discreet, but had the same wandering eyes. A short time ago, he was just what she looked for. A little, old married man who was willing to pay good money for the opportunity to lay his head against the soft, warm flesh of another woman's bosom, heck, they didn't even want nothing more than a few moments of having their head cradled deep in the cleavage between the two.

When the old lady closed her eyes, Delores even found herself flaunting her assets, as she saw the old man squirm in his seat. Delores had enjoyed those encounters rather than the wham-bam-thank-ya-ma'am rough, and unwashed cowboys who just wanted a few minutes of enjoyment. You always had to be careful as to who you serviced. Many a prostitute found herself with a black eye or blooded lip or even worse. Most of the prostitutes had no families and went by nicknames anyways such as Big Nose Kate who was famous as Doc Holiday's woman. He was known to slap her around some and yet she followed him wherever he went. A lot of these Soiled Doves were young Chinese girls who came over here as mail order brides, only to be forced into prostitution in order to survive. No one paid attention to a prostitute being beat up, raped, or even murdered. There are as many of these women in Boot Hill Cemeteries as there are men. Her own sister being one of them who was raped and no justice was given to the man who did it because he was well known.

And now, standing on the boardwalk of this western town, her gaze fell on the black man, dressed in black standing, watching them get off the stage. Delores tapped her sister on the shoulder and indicated she was headed in his direction.

CHAPTER 8

The first slivers of sunlight turned the morning sky into all shades of reds, pinks, oranges, blues and golden yellows so bright they hurt your eyes to look at it.

The night had passed quickly for Sam. The chirping of a few birds were welcome sounds to his ears. The night had been one where the only sounds heard were those coming from his creaking saddle and the constant clop, clop of his mount's footsteps on the hard, packed trail. But it wasn't these sounds that got his attention now but, the smell of smoke and coffee.

"Could it be?" he questioned in his mind.

Sam nudged his horse off the trail towards the thin gray spiral of smoke he saw when he looked in the direction of the smell.

"Hello the camp." Sam addressed it as he came in sight of it and spied a lone figure of a man sitting next to a small fire.

Sam was close enough to recognize Harry's face as he looked in the direction of his voice and a smile lit up his face.

"What in the blazes are you doing out here?" Harry asked. A look of surprise on his face at seeing who it was riding into his camp.

"Probably saving your hide," Sam answered.

"Well, get down and grab a cup of coffee and tell me all about it." Harry said, already heading for his saddle bag to get another metal cup for his friend.

"Holy crap!" came a loud report from Sam's mouth with the first swallow of coffee.

"What in the tarnation is the stuff you're drinking?"

"I never could make a good cup of coffee," he told Sam "Have a tendency to make it a little strong."

"A little strong is an understatement, wouldn't you say, Harry?"

Sam picked up the pot and opened the lid and looked inside. Pouring some more water in it he sat it back on the hot cools to get it to boiling again.

"Slade's in Cripple Creek," he finally said. "He's with another man they call Reverend or Crow."

"Crow!" exclaimed Harry.

"The locals call him Reverend, but I was told he also goes by the name Crow. By your reaction, you know the name?"

"Crow is as bad if not worse than Slade," he told Sam, "More of a cold blooded killer."

"He works for Slade who owns a ranch, not too far out of town."

"I take it you haven't secured Slade yet?" was Harry's next question.

"No I haven't, Harry."

"The tone of your voice and you being here tells me there's more to this story."

"I killed one of Slade's men." Sam told him. His voice a whisper.

The morning sky had given way from its brilliant reds to a soft shade of blue. Much different than the rain filled one he had ridden from. The aroma of boiling coffee in the air, indicated to Sam that it was ready. Dumping what remained in his cup onto the ground, he poured another cup before offering the pot to Harry.

"Much better," he said, taking a sip of the hot liquid.

"Much better," Harry agreed, taking a sip of his. "How'd you do that?"

"Simple. Next time you make a pot, use about half the coffee you normally do."

"Now, tell me about this man you killed."

"Not much to tell, Harry." He said. "This Slade fella, like owns the town and he had found out about me being in town. Seems he doesn't like strangers there. He had sent one of his men to find me. I was in the livery stable getting information from the owner when one of Slade's men approached. He was about to do harm to the livery, so I shot him from the hiding place I was in."

As they finished their coffee, Sam finished telling his story.

"I'm sure we can't go into town without being noticed. Slade would for sure have men keeping an eye out for anyone riding into town now," he told Harry. "Slade had men before that let him know when anyone new came to town."

"The fella you shot. What did you do with his body?"

"I dragged him out of town and pushed him down a ravine about two miles out of town," Sam told him, "It was raining so hard I figured there would be no tracks to follow. Would imagine some wild animals have found him by now."

"You said Slade had a ranch in Cripple Creek?" questioned Harry, trying to put some kind of plan together.

"About three miles out of town to the west, I was told."

"Is there a way around Cripple Creek, so we can get to his ranch without having to pass through it?" Harry asked.

Sam noticed that Harry had picked up a stick and was marking some things on the ground. A makeshift sort of map.

"I think about three hours back, I passed a fork in the road. Being black out, couldn't really tell, Harry."

"Was the fork to the north or south?" Harry asked. He drew in a fork going to the north when Sam told him that.

"You can't say for sure if you were followed out of town or not?"

"No I can't, Harry. But I wouldn't think I was, at least not then. Now come sun-up." Sam hunched his shoulders, in a visual question mark.

"For now looks like we will take that fork. We can't take a chance of running into any of Slade's men although he probably would have some kind of look-out person on any trail that could possibly be a threat to him."

Sam stomped out the fire as Harry saddled Jake. Plans were to take the fork and hopefully run into someone who wasn't one of Slade's men who could give them an idea as to their location.

Sam and Harry for the most part rode in silence and before long, it did come to a fork in the trail. The forked trail was nicely used, so Harry figured it would lead them to another town, an assumption that was correct. That town, being Pleasant Pines, was also about sixty miles northwest, a distance he couldn't have known, for if he had, he probably wouldn't have taken it.

Morning soon turned into high noon and the sun's rays had both men wanting some fresh water and something to eat. Coming across a small creek bed, they reined up so that the horses could drink and they also decided to rest a short bit. Harry took a couple of cans from his saddle bags and tossed one to Sam.

"Peaches," he said. "All I brought. Figured to be in Cripple Creek today, so didn't plan on trail food."

"So. What's the plan, Harry?" Sam asked, plopping a slice of peach into his mouth. It's rich flavor attacking his taste buds.

"You said that Slade's ranch was due west of Cripple Creek. We are headed northwest, which will put us above his ranch, but where above we don't know, and won't know till we come across a town or someone who can tell us." Thinking for a moment he continued. "Knowing his ranch is located here is troubling."

"Why is that?" asked Sam.

"I was hoping to catch him in town or on the trail someplace. Now, he will be held up on his ranch surrounded by his armed men, so there will be no way to get to him," Harry replied, now having to re-think all other plans. "I was really hoping you would have him under lock and key, by the time I showed up."

"I was hoping the same thing, Harry. Now I'm beginning to wonder if it's a lost cause at this time. He knows there is at least one person looking for him, and like you said, he will be holed up on his ranch where he has his protection. It will be impossible to get at him."

One thing the two noticed was the difference in the terrain. It had become rocky, steep and there were Evergreen trees everywhere.

"It would appear we are coming into hill country," Harry remarked.

"Sure does," acknowledged Sam. "The temperature has changed some."

Another hour and the traces of smoke was in the air.

"Do you smell smoke?" Harry asked, reining Duke to a halt.

"Sure do," came Sam's reply, "and it's getting stronger."

Half a mile further, the trail turned into the main street of a little hole-in-the-wall establishment known as Pleasant Pines.

Pleasant Pines was made up of a saloon, a hotel with a couple of gaming tables, a mercantile store, a livery/freight hauling business and an eating place called Millie's.

Dismounting in front of the livery, Harry and Sam went inside in hopes of finding someone who could give them some information. The figure of a man who met them inside was just what Harry had visualized. The man was about six feet four and built like a mountain. Unkempt beard, hair and an old ragged pair of overalls with only one strap slung over his shoulder.

"Howdy," Harry said nodding his head slightly.

"Howdy," came the reply. "You gents want something?"

"Some feed for our horses and some information as to where we are. We're headed to Cripple Creek," Harry answered.

"Feed for the horses will be two-bits apiece. As for Cripple Creek, you should have stayed on the main road you came off of at the fork," he told them.

"Do we need to go back or does this trail turn-up there?"

Both Sam and Harry saw the slight grin come across his face as he spoke.

"This road goes all the way to Silver Springs," he told them. "But it is a good day's ride from here, then another half-a-day's ride from there. I'd suggest you go back the way you came and get on the main trail. Save you about half-day of travel."

Harry reached into his pocket and pulled out the coins needed to feed their horses.

"One more question," he asked dropping the coins into the livery's out-stretched hand. "How's the grub at Millie's?"

"Anything but the steak. Sometimes it's a little old. Bacon and eggs, home fried potatoes, corn bread, coffee would be my suggestion."

Smacking his lips, Sam remarked. "Sounds tasty to me. Would you like to join us?"

"Thanks for the offer, mister, but I'm good."

Bacon and eggs was a good choice indeed. A second cup of coffee and a slice of pie was the finishing to a good meal.

"It's a day's ride from here to Silver Springs. What do you suggest we do? Stay here and make the ride tomorrow, or continue and sleep out under the stars tonight?"

"Let's get some food to take with us, along with a pouch of coffee and hit the trail. We can knock off a half-day of travel by doing so."

Once they had finished, they went to the mercantile and picked up a few canned goods along with a pouch of coffee.

"You're the coffee maker," Harry jokingly said to Sam.

"Fine by me," Sam said back. "I've tasted your coffee!"

The livery had fed the horses, removed their saddles, and given them both a good rub down. Once saddled, Harry and Sam thanked him and proceeded on their way, but not before being warned to look out for black bear and a couple of mountain lions prowling about.

"I'm glad you decided to hit the trail instead of staying in town, Harry. There are a couple of things I want to talk to you about," Sam told him.

The terrain had leveled off and the trail was surprisingly smooth, so they were able to proceed at a brisk pace. Their mounts were more than happy to comply with the pace, and both Sam and Harry were soon feeling the strain of the ride. The trail was such that they rode in single file for the most part having taken a short-cut trail they were told about. Although it wouldn't save them a lot of time, but any would help.

The afternoon went by quickly and soon the sky started to take on the colors of evening. Up ahead, they saw the site they had been told about that was good to set up camp. A small area surrounded by huge boulders and plenty of dead wood for a fire. Someone long ago had built an impressive fire pit and surrounded it with tree stumps to act as seating. There was also some firewood stacked around it.

It became quickly obvious where the horses were bedded, by the odor of horse droppings. Soon there was a fire burning and the smell of boiling coffee filled the night's air. True to his words, Sam made the coffee and Harry had to agree, it was some of the best he had experienced.

"What did you want to talk about earlier?" Harry asked.

A far away, owww, owww, owooooah of a coyote singing his evening song filled the now darkened sky.

"You know Harry, I was a US Marshal at one time before leaving the department and becoming a bounty hunter, yet I don't think I ever put aside being a marshal." Sam stopped to sip his coffee then continued.

"Meeting you has set my mind to thinking about re-joining the US Marshals. What do you think my chances are of being hired again?"

Harry stared at Sam, listening intensely to what he was saying and knew he was serious.

Before Harry could remark, Sam continued.

"I've been able to put away a large sum of money and if I am able to turn Slade in, well, that will set me. I want to find me the right woman and settle down. As much as I enjoy being on the open trail, I could enjoy it more if I had a woman to return to. I'm still young enough to start a family even."

Harry knew all about what Sam was saying. Even now his thoughts were on Amanda and the past couple of days they had enjoyed each other.

"You killed a man, a day back, protecting the lives of two others. You high-tailed out of there to stop me from riding into what would surely of lead to my getting killed. You're still a lawman inside and there is no denying that. If you're really serious about coming back into the organization, I'll do everything I can to help make that happen."

Harry's plans were to stay out here in the west with Amanda and he would be needing a good partner and Sam would make a good partner, but first things first.

"That's more than I can ask for, Harry." Sam said.

"First things first, though. We have a Slade matter to take care of, and that is one I've given lots of thought to, as we rode along. The way I look at it, we have to get Slade off his ranch and preferably alone, which we both know isn't going to happen. As you have witnessed, he rides with some of his men."

"So, what's the plan, Harry? I told you about the Reverend. For sure Slade will keep him by his side. I can't even see him leaving his ranch now."

"When we get to Silver Springs, I'm thinking we will probably find out that at least one, if not more, of Slade's men will be there just checking and asking questions concerning you. He will for sure have look-outs in Cripple Creek."

"Maybe we need to put Slade on hold till a later time when all this has quieted down and he isn't on guard."

Sam's statement he knew wasn't going to be taken seriously by Harry. Heck, he didn't take it seriously himself. Neither Harry nor Sam were aware a surprisingly change of events was about to take place.

CHAPTER 9

The remainder of the trip to Silver Springs was uneventful. No black bears or mountain lions, just the never ending clop, clop of horse hooves against hard ground. It was decided that Harry would enter Silver Springs by himself, just in case Slade has a look-out there who might recognize Sam's face.

"I'll check things out and speak to the sheriff if they have one," it was decided on by Harry.

When they first smelled signs of smoke they looked around for a good place for Sam to hold up till he returned.

Harry would normally search out the livery to get Duke taken care of but also knew it would be a good place for a lookout person, so he entered Silver Springs and scoped out the town for a sheriff's office. Harry was amazed at the size of Silver Springs. There were several streets that intersected with a town square which housed a court house/sheriff's office, two churches, several saloons and eateries along with a few hotels. All kinds of shops lined the several streets of town.

Even from a distance one could hear the hustle and bustle coming from the saloons and the patrons moving about in the streets. Harry was hoping his arrival would be unannounced, but after seeing all the people, he felt his presence probably didn't go unnoticed.

The sheriff's name was Harlan Calhoun and he actually seemed happy to meet Harry. After Harry explained why he was there, Harlan seemed relieved.

"That explains why those two men are here," Harlan told Harry. "Yesterday a black man dressed in black and another young buck sporting a low slung rig came into town. The black man went by the name Reverend and his partner simply KC."

"I take it they are still in town?" Harry asked.

"Yes, sir. That Reverend fella is over at the Silver Spring saloon and gambling emporium and has a room at that same hotel. The other fella spends his time lounging around the livery and I was told spent the night there in one of the empty stalls."

Harry knew that he and Sam would have to deal with these two. He had never heard of the fella named KC, but had heard of the Reverend who went by the name Crow and he was a gunslinger, a cold bloody murderer.

"I have a plan, sheriff, but will need your help. I don't want to get anyone killed but that will be up to them. Can I count on you?"

"You sure can, Harry. But," he warned, "don't look for a lot of help from the town folk. Slade and his men drop a lot of money between here and Cripple Creek and he owns the Silver Spring Saloon."

Harry glanced out of the sheriff's office window, just as the Overland Stage Coach pulled into town. As it approached the stage depot, Harry also saw the Reverend step from the Silver Spring Saloon and watched who might get off the stage. Harry watched as six passengers disembarked. His eyes moving between the Reverend and the passengers.

He watched in disbelief as two women dressed in brightly colored dresses stepped out of the coach and onto the boardwalk, stopping to turn around to get a look at the town. If they could have seen inside the window, they would have met the eyes of US Marshal Harry Finch. Harry watched as the two sisters walked down and seemingly introduced themselves to the big black man. A couple minutes later, they followed him back into the Silver Spring Saloon.

"I need to find out what those two are doing here," Harry thought.

Turning from the window he faced Harlan and asked.

"Harlan, I need your help in a very delicate matter."

"Anything I can help you with, you only need to ask," he told Harry. "Anything, just ask."

"Two women, or better yet, sisters just got off the stage and approached the Reverend. Moments later, they left with him and entered the saloon. I need to speak with the one called Delores. Her sister is Bridget and I need you to help make that happen."

"Ask for Delores Avery, tell her you need to speak with her in private, in regards to a Charles Freeman," he told the sheriff. "I won't tell you more so you have no more information to give, if she questions you. Just get her to come back here with you. I'll be in the back room waiting."

Harlan took his broad brimmed Stetson from the hat hook, adjusted it on his head then headed across the street to the Silver Spring Saloon as Harry waited, hoping that his plan worked.

Inside the Silver Springs, Harlan spotted the two women and the Reverend sitting at a corner table away from the rest. As he neared their table, he saw the Reverend stare at him and his eye brows lift. Stepping up to their table, Harlan tipped his hat in a welcome gesture.

"Good afternoon folks," he said, before asking. "Are either one of you a Delores Avery?"

Both sisters looked up at the mention of Delores' name.

"I'm Delores Avery," she spoke.

Harlan saw the questioning look on her face and the cold, bloody stare coming from the Reverend, which stood the short hairs on Harlan's neck up.

"I need to have a private word with you, Miss Avery, concerning a Charles Freeman."

"What about Mr. Freeman?" Bridget interrupted.

"I just need to speak to Miss Avery, ma'am." Harlan could see that he had encountered a snag in Harry's plan and needed to come up with an alternate.

"I'm her sister, Bridget. If you need to speak to her, you can also speak with me."

It was a statement, accompanied by her standing and facing him.

"Well, if Miss Avery says it is okay, that's fine seeing you're sisters and all."

Not exactly as planned Harry but will have to do, were his thoughts as Delores stood and said, "It's okay, let's go."

Harry was looking out the window when Harlan and, to his surprise, both sisters emerged from the saloon. They were also followed by the Reverend, but he stopped and stood outside watching them. Just before they reached the office, Harry stepped into the other room, out of sight.

As the three entered his office, Harlan motioned for them to have a seat. Instead of sitting as indicated, a very irate Delores demanded to know what this was all about.

"I'll answer that." Harry's voice came from behind them, giving them a start.

Turning, both sisters gave an audible gasp of surprise at seeing US Marshal Harry Finch standing there.

"Well, well. If it isn't Harry Finch," said Delores. "I told you we would meet again."

Gone was the earlier sharpness in her voice, replaced with one of recognition and questioning. Harry, stepping up to the window, looked out to see if the Reverend was still outside. He was.

"What are you doing here?" Harry's voice asked demandingly.

"I could ask you the same thing." Was the answer he received.

"No time to explain now," said Harry, "but we need to talk. It's very important, and we need to be alone."

"Tomorrow we take the stage to Cripple Creek. Why don't we meet there?"

"We need to talk before then," replied Harry. "The stage will have to make a couple stops on the way."

"There's a stage stop about ten miles from here," Harlan informed them.

"Great. We'll meet you there. In the meantime, don't tell anyone about this, especially the Reverend," Harry warned the two.

"You'd best get back now. Remember, tell no one," Harry warned again.

One last glance out the window, Harry saw the Reverend still standing, waiting for the two to return.

"What makes you think we will do anything you say, Harry?" questioned Bridget.

"You want to live. Don't you?" was Harry's reply.

"The Reverend is going to get suspicious if you don't get back," said Harry. "And please listen to me on this without question. I'll make it very clear, when we meet."

One last glance out the window, and Harry stepped into the back room ending any further conversation.

Harlan turned and opened the door and said, "I'll walk you back and give you some cover so you won't get questioned by that Reverend fella," then in a whispered voice told them. "He's a bad one. A killer."

As they approached the spot where the Reverend stood, Harlan tipped his hat and apologized.

"I'm truly sorry for the misunderstanding on that Charlie Freeman issue ma'am, he said before turning and walking back towards his office.

As Harry watched from the window, he was hoping the two sisters would trust him and not mention anything to the Reverend about their meeting here or the one planned for later. Harry needed to leave now to get back with Sam and put a plan together, although he had given some thought to Sam's remark about letting this go till a later time. It was plain to see Slade expected some kind of trouble, and maybe it would be best to wait awhile. But Harry was a US Marshal on a mission and wouldn't be deferred from it no matter what obstacles were thrown in his path. Harry's hopes now were to get out of town the same way he arrived. Unseen!

"I'll get your horse and meet you out back," Harlan offered. "The alley leads all the way to the edge of town and no one should see you."

"Thanks a lot for all your help, Sheriff," Harry said, extending his hand.

"Glad I could help out, Marshal," came his reply, followed by a strong grasp of his extended hand.

As far as Harry knew, no one saw him leave. As he rode, he kept going over the day's affair. Harry soon arrived at the spot where he had left Sam. His horse was there along with a fire where he spied a pot of coffee boiling, but no Sam.

His concern for the moment ended when Sam stepped out from behind one of the large boulders which surrounded the site.

"Figured it would be about time you be getting back," he said, as Harry stepped down off Duke's back. "Fresh pot of Joe just for you." He pointed toward the pot and even handed Harry his metal coffee cup.

Moments later, Harry was sipping his coffee and relaying the happenings he experienced in Silver Springs.

"The sisters didn't tell you anything?" he asked, surprised when Harry told him they were in Silver Springs.

"We didn't have time to talk because of a black man, known as the Reverend, was outside watching. So, we set a place where we could meet them. The sheriff told me of a stage stop half way between here and Cripple Creek, so that will be where we'll meet unless something else comes up. He also told me how to get around the town."

"Who is this Reverend you just mentioned?"

"Well, Reverend is the name he goes by out here. I recognized him from a poster as a murdering gunman known as Crow."

At the word 'poster,' Sam's eyes widened.

"There is a bounty on him?" Sam questioned.

"Yes, there is," Harry told him. "You will be a very rich man if all goes as planned and we can get both him and Slade. Seeing I can't claim the bounty, I'll give you the credit for their capture."

"How much was his bounty?" a now excited Sam asked.

"I don't recall, except it was a lot," Harry replied.

Let's get your horse saddled, put out that fire, and head on out. I want to be at that stage stop before sundown. We will have to ride hard to make that happen."

Plans that Harry had before now changed with the Avery sisters obviously entering the picture. He would have to wait and see exactly what they were doing here.

"You weren't kidding when you said we needed to ride hard to make the stage stop before sundown," Sam remarked when they stopped later on in the day to water their horses.

The stage stop was located at a little ghost town by the name of Dry Creek. It was a much needed stop, if you were traveling between Silver Springs and Cripple Creek.

M and M Livery and Dry Goods was the name of the stop. It was owned by a middle aged couple named Marty and Maranda. Harry learned that the stage they would meet tomorrow only came through twice a week since the town died.

"You're looking at someone else's dream when you look at the M and M." Marty told Harry as they sat about jawing over a piece of Maranda's apple pie and fresh coffee.

Sam was out and about checking the empty buildings which used to make up Dry Creek.

"Used to be a busy stop, not only for the stage, but also for the lone traveler, seeing how it fell half-way between Cripple Creek and Silver Springs. Short time ago, the stage ran every other day. As Cripple Creek and Silver Springs grew, travel east to west grew and north to south died with that, so did the town."

"But you and Maranda stayed on?" Harry questioned. "Why?"

"Maranda and I don't need much. The stage and the one or two travelers passing through during the week keeps us happy."

"But how do you run this place on so little?" Was Harry's next question.

Here, a smile lit up Marty's face as he started to speak.

"The town is still a registered town. So I elected myself mayor and sheriff of Dry Creek and believe it or not draw a small salary from the state. Now ain't that something," he told Harry, slapping his knee and busting out laughing.

Harry had to agree, that sure was something, as he joined in the laughter.

After their good laugh, Marty ask what brought them to Dry Creek.

"You seem too polished to just be a cowboy passing through," he remarked. "You seem more of a lawman than anything."

"Why would you think that I am a lawman?" Harry asked, intrigued by his sharp observation.

"Don't take much for a man to read another, if he pays attention," Harry was told.

"So, Marty tell me what do you read?" Harry asked him. "What do you see?"

"Well, to start, you ride a nice horse, then there are the clothes. You say you two have been riding hard, but your clothes don't show it, telling me they're expensive. You wear that sidearm strapped down but not low slung like a gunfighter would. The way you speak. That's not cowboy lingo. No. My guess a lawman. But your friend. He is a gunfighter. No one wears a strapped down low slung rig, if he doesn't mean business. Riding with you, I'd say he was a bounty hunter."

If a man could read another man, you could read the amazed look on Harry's face.

"I'm hoping I can trust you, and I think I can read that in you," Harry stated. "You called it pretty accurate. I'm a US Marshal and my friend is indeed a bounty hunter."

"What brings you two through here, Marshal?"

Before Harry could answer, Maranda hollered out from the front door that supper was awaiting.

Marty looked at Harry then told him, "Don't expect much to eat tonight because the stage comes through tomorrow and we save everything for then, never knowing how many will be on the stage.

Harry was just about to say something, when he heard his name.

"Harry!" The loud voice of Sam yelled from behind him.

Turning to face the voice, Harry saw two others walking with him and one was a kid.

"Remember that livery guy who hid me before I had to kill one of Slade's men. Well, this is Joe, the livery owner and his boy."

"Are you really a US Marshal?" asked the boy. His voice filled with excitement at having met a real to life US Marshal.

Nodding his head, Harry reached out his hand to the boy.

"I'm US Marshal Harry Finch," he told the boy who eagerly grabbed his outstretched hand.

I'm Walter," he introduced himself, "but everyone calls me Walt."

"Well, Walt. Glade to meet you. I'm Harry Finch." Thinking, Harry continued, "Most folk simply call me Marshal."

"I'm Joe, Marshal. Sam here has told me a lot about you."

"He has? Well I hope it was all good stuff," Harry glanced over at Sam, just as Marty told them, "Let's go eat!"

As they sat around the table eating a simple stew, Marty started telling them about a black gunslinger who came through yesterday looking for any strangers and also the livery, Joe.

"You said you could read a man, is that why you called him a gunslinger?" Harry asked.

"That and him buying a box of shells and firing off every one out back where he had sat up some cans. Lightning fast he is, but can't hit crap from fifty feet out."

That was good news to Harry's ears. Harry now knew his weak spot if they ever came face to face. Supper done, Harry told Sam that they needed to get some sleep, so they made their way to the abandoned hotel where they both took a room overlooking the street where the stage stop was located.

In the morning they would tell Marty and Maranda who to expect on the stage. Harry fell asleep hoping the Reverend wasn't riding with them.

CHAPTER 10

After a restless night of little sleep, the golden slivers of morning sun came in through the window, greeting Harry to a new day. A day filled with uncertainties. It took Harry a couple of minutes to adjust to where he was. The abandoned hotel had a smell of decay such as Harry had never smelled before. Harry left his room and knocked on Sam's door.

"It's open," came Sam's voice, through the quietness of the abandoned hotel.

Harry found Sam sitting on the edge of his bed. He had pulled over the night stand and had his pistol all apart and was in the process of cleaning it.

"Tools of the trade," he told Harry. "I do this every morning regardless if I fire it or not."

Sam spoke without looking up from what he was doing. "Have a plan, Harry?"

"The only plan I have concerns the Reverend and only if he shows up. Can't really go beyond there until I speak with the sisters. Everything rides on their story as to why they have showed up here and what their business is with the Reverend."

As Harry spoke, Sam was trying to remember what the sister Bridget looked like, but couldn't see her in his memories. He just remembered her as being the prettiest woman he had ever laid eyes on.

"What's your plan if the Reverend does show up?" Sam asked, finishing the assembly of his pistol, reloading it and dropping it into the well-oiled holster strapped to his waist.

"According to my conversation with Marty, I was told that he is lightning fast on the draw but couldn't hit a barn door if it was fifty feet away, so I plan on staying that distance away from him no matter what. And the more I think about it, I'd like him to ride in here where we can get him alone, away from all the others. We could eliminate one of Slade's top gunmen at least."

"That all sounds swell as long as what Marty observed is true. After all, you're a lot smaller than a barn door," Sam said with a smile on his face.

"Let's go get a coffee. I need to talk to Marty and his wife, before the stage arrives. I'm going to tell him what he might expect if the Reverend shows up."

Not only did Maranda have a large pot of coffee made, but a small spread of biscuits and bacon.

"Stage usually arrives around eleven-twenty," Marty told Harry, motioning for them both to help themselves.

When they finished, Harry followed Marty outside.

"I need to talk with you about what could transpire here today with the arrival of the stage," he began. "If the

Reverend shows up there is without a doubt going to be some bloodshed. I need you and Maranda to stay inside, if shooting begins. I can't be worrying about either one you."

"So, I was right about the Reverend being a gunslinger," Marty stated as Harry continued. "I will confront him outside and going by what you told me, I plan on stepping out of your barn which I stepped off earlier as being fifty-seven feet or so from the front of the doorway."

"That distance is approximate and watching him, he knows his limitations and if confronted outside, he will make sure he closes that gap before any gun play." Marty advised.

"Seven feet. Three steps. How do you plan on stopping him from taking those three steps?"

Marty had a point. Harry knew that Reverend would easily be able to move even closer, knowing he wouldn't draw first being a lawman.

"I'll figure it out," Harry spoke. But even as he did, Marty saw the look of concern on Harry's face.

Just then Sam stepped outside and joined in the conversation.

"Have a plan put together yet?" asked Sam.

"Working on it, Sam."

As he spoke, Sam quickly drew his sidearm. As he did he said, "Why don't I just face him down? I want the bounty anyways."

"That's it!" Harry said.

Marty picked up a different tone in his statement and asked Harry to explain.

"Not now. Sam let's go for a walk, so I can work this all out." he said, grabbing Sam by the arm and headed down the street of the abandoned town.

Harry decided if the Reverend did ride into town he would confront him right away and hope that it would catch him somewhat off-guard and maybe give him the edge he would need to come out on top.

Just about eleven o'clock, Harry and Sam took up their locations to wait for the stage.

At eleven-twenty exactly he heard the far away sounds of the stage and stepped back into the barn out of the doorway but within view of the front of the stage stop.

As the stage pulled into view engulfed in a cloud of dust, Harry noticed the lone rider following it. The lone rider being the Reverend.

Harry now could only hope his plan worked. It was a solid plan, so Harry took a deep breath, checked his Colt out of habit and watched as the stage came to a stop.

There were only two passengers that got off the stage, and it was Delores and Bridget.

The Reverend tied his horse to the tie bar on the back of the coach and opened the stage's door and offered a hand to Dolores who was the first to step out, then Bridget. Both sisters were dressed in brightly colored, frilly dresses which radiated in the noon sun.

Right away, Harry saw the flaw in his plan. The stage coach was in the way. If I call him out it will be easy for him to walk to the front of the team putting him within his known kill zone. What to do now? Harry's mind was racing as well as his heart. Knowing his day probably wasn't going to end well, Harry stepped from the barn.

"Reverend!" Harry called out. His voice and Reverend's name stopping all three who were walking towards the front door of the stage depot.

At this distance, Harry could easily see the face of the Reverend was cold and blank. Harry had been right for he now saw the Reverend start to walk towards him to get past the team of horses, which would place him well within the fifty feet distance.

BOOM, BOOM! Came the loud report from a double barreled shotgun.

Harry watched the Reverend's eyes bulge out, as his chest exploded out through his shirt as his body was flung forward taking the blast from the double barrel shot gun and landed face down on the ground in a cloud of dust.

In the doorway of the depot stood Maranda, holding the still smoking shotgun. They would all learn, even her husband Marty, the Reverend had raped her when he came thru two days ago. The outcome of this encounter had turned out completely different than Harry expected or had planned. Both Marty and Maranda refused any reward for the Reverend, so Sam would take the credit and collect the reward money.

'One more to go' was Sam's thoughts as dollar signs floated around in his head.

The stage driver and Sam hauled the Reverend's body to the abandoned town cemetery and dug him a grave in the Boot Hill section. No casket, just a body rolled up in an old tarp and dumped into a hole in the ground and covered with dirt. This being the fate of many a gunfighter. That taken care of, the next line of business was to speak with the two sisters.

Harry showed his credentials to the stage driver and told him it would be a couple of hours before he could leave. Harry instructed Marty to help him with the team, while he waited.

After learning what business the sisters were going to conduct with Slade as far as hiring him to kill the man who had raped Bridget, Harry quickly put together a plan.

"We will need to get Slade here, where we can take him down. I will need you Sam, to ride hard back to Silver Springs and get the sheriff here immediately. See if you can locate Joe also and bring him along. Tell them we need help bringing Slade in. The sheriff knows the story and he also knows about you. Bridget and Dolores will travel to Cripple Creek and will get word to Slade as to what transpired here today and to tell him the Reverend is dead."

"Anyone want coffee," it was Maranda.

"We're all set for now," Harry told her. "Thank you."

Harry then continued on with his plan.

"Delores will tell him that the US Marshal is also waiting here for him. He will no doubt come here, but with his men. I will be watching from the trail to see just how many that will be. Two are already dead, so it shouldn't be more than five or six. As soon as I know, I will ride back here and wait for their arrival. Providing you get the sheriff, we will have four."

"Six," it was Maranda's voice. "Six counting me and Marty.

"I can't ask you to do this," Harry said.

"You didn't ask, we volunteer," Maranda said.

"Well, we want in on this to," Delores spoke up.

"No, Delores. I want you two to stay in Cripple Creek. When this is over, we will meet you there."

"Who gets to claim the bounty?" Sam asked, in a concerned voice. "You know I came here to claim that bounty."

"We don't need to be worrying about that right now," Harry told him. "Let's see what happens here."

All agreed and soon the stage with Delores and Bridget rolled out from the M and M stage stop and headed to Cripple Creek.

Sam saddled up and headed back to Silver Springs and Harry decided he would ride a ways in the stage to get to know the two sisters more. They told him what had happened in Eastman and to their old friend, Dusty Wade. All three learned a lot about each other during that ride.

Harry got some laughs whenever the stage hit a hole and bounced the two sisters into the air and listened to their "Oweeeeee" as their bottoms smacked back down on the stage's hard seat.

"You say you're going to be headed to San Francisco?" Harry asked Delores. "And what are you going to do, Bridget?" Having been told that they would be separating for a while.

"I thought I knew, but now not so sure," she told him.

The afternoon went by quickly and soon the driver brought the stage to a halt and informed Harry that Cripple Creek was only a mile away.

"Pretty sure that nothing major will happen tonight. Get checked into the hotel and wait till morning, before starting to inquire about Slade. Sam told me that the people there were connected to him, so word will travel quickly to him especially if you mention the Reverend," Harry said.

The stage driver told Harry of a couple places on the trail from Cripple Creek to Slade's ranch where he could have an advantage point to overlook the trail without being observed. He would miss his coffee in the morning, but couldn't take a chance on a fire, as there was no way of telling when someone would be passing through.

The three miles from Cripple Creek to Slade's ranch could be covered quickly by a lone rider, and that lone rider went galloping past at eight o'clock, the next morning. The same rider returned, followed by a person who Harry recognized as Slade himself, along with five others.

"Total of seven," Harry said out loud. "If Sam returns with the sheriff and Joe, the number would be six to seven. Pretty even if you ask me." He continued talking, more to reassure himself than anything else.

"Sometimes when you speak out loud and hear yourself, things make more sense, sometimes less."

Harry now headed back to the M and M stage station, hoping Sam was able to retain the services of the sheriff and Joe. When Harry returned to the M and M stage stop, he found it boarded up and was met by Marty who stepped from the barn.

"Sam, the sheriff and Joe arrived a short time ago," he told Harry. "Everyone is in the abandoned saloon waiting for you. How many are there?" he asked.

"Seven," came Harry's reply "But let's wait until we are all together so I can tell everyone."

It was good to see the sheriff and Joe, when Harry entered the saloon. Marty and Maranda had supplied a couple of bottles of Rye and one was almost gone. An empty glass was filled and handed to Harry when he entered.

"There are six men riding this way with Slade," he told them. "I'm not sure of the time when they will arrive, but it looks like we'll be ready.'

Downing his drink, he was offered another, but refused.

"Let's spread out and take up different locations, that way we will have a better chance when the gun play begins. As soon as they dismount, I'm gonna call Spade out from the far end of town. Each one of you, pick a target to go after once the shooting begins. Hopefully, they won't be so anxious to fight, if they see Slade face down in the street."

"You have no way of knowing that for sure and if by chance Slade was to kill you we would be without a leader. I suggest you let me challenge him. When I draw my piece, I hit what's in front of me," Sam said.

"Sam has a point, Harry," said the sheriff from Silver Springs. "We need you alive."

As much as Harry was against this new plan, he had to admit in case he was shot, the others would be without his leadership and at Slade's mercy.

Everyone took up different places and waited. Their wait was short. Soon the pounding sound of galloping horse's hooves against the hard trail told everyone the time had arrived. Hearts pounded in their chests at the sight of seven cowboys galloping to the stage stop. For a few seconds, the cloud of dust obscured them from sight. When the dust cloud cleared, all seven were on the ground and standing in front of the M and M.

"Slade." Sam's voice split the afternoon air and fourteen sets of eyes turned towards the sound of it. Guns were drawn and ready for trouble.

All eyes watched as Slade motioned for his men to hold tight. As he stepped away from the stage stop and into the street of the abandoned town, he started to walk toward the figure of Sam, who stood at the opposite end of town.

As he got closer, Sam yelled out, "Far enough, Slade."

Slade stopped for a second, before continuing.

"Far enough," Sam yelled again.

"One more step and you best be drawing your weapon." Sam warned tor the last time.

Sam readied himself to draw no matter what happened next. He knew Slade would take that next step and as soon as he made a move, he would be shooting.

Slade sensed what would happen next. As he lifted his foot in start of stepping, he drew his pistol at the same time and fired at Sam.

As he fired, Slade saw the white puff of smoke come from the end of Sam's drawn sidearm, but never felt the bullet that tore through his chest, exploded his heart, and exited through his back. All eyes on Slade, no one saw Sam fall to the ground also.

The next shot to be heard was that of Harry's gun being shot into the dirt, next to where Slade's men stood. He and Maranda had stepped out of the barn. Maranda had her shotgun leveled at the seven and was cocked and ready to fire, but there was no need.

As Harry had suspected, once Slade was dead they wouldn't fight.

With their hands in the air and their weapons on the ground, those in the abandoned buildings came out, relieved that there was no other shooting to be done. Joe was the first to see Sam and hollered to the others.

Rushing to Sam, Joe saw the trickle of blood on his cheek. Slade's bullet had grazed the side of his head and had removed a portion of his right ear, but he was alive and would live.

The day ended with another hole being dug in the Boot Hill section of the abandoned cemetery.

This being the mortal ending to most gunfighter's lives. A hole in the ground as they have their, 'Rendezvous with Boot Hill'

THE END

Epilogue

The happenings of that day at the M and M stage stop had lasting effects on several of those that were there.

Several of Slade's men were wanted by the law and had small bounties on them, which was collected and divided amongst them.

Joe and his boy went back to his livery business, but sold out and moved to Silver Springs. He bought the livery plus the blacksmith business because the owner wanted to move to Arizona.

Marty and Maranda re-opened the hotel and the saloon and changed the name of the abandoned town to Twin Pines. The past was never brought up again.

Delores continued on by herself to San Francisco where she met and fell in love with a school teacher. She never pursued having Charles Freeman killed, but learned from her sister that he went to prison for the rape of another woman.

Bridget stayed on to nurse Sam back to health. When he was healed, he and Bridget were married.

Sam and Bridget made their home in Silver Springs, where Bridget would become a doctor and open her own practice. Sam, with Harry's help, was welcomed back and became a US Marshal. He would go on to receive several commendations. He and Harry would join forces many times to bring in the bad guys.

And Harry. Well, he returned to Amanda whom he married. He closed down his Washington, D.C. office and relocated to Thunder Point, where he and Amanda started that family he had only dreamed about.

Harry was instrumental in Sam's return to the US Marshals, and on several occasions would work together again in the future.

The Harry Finch Western Series are short stories he told to his grandkids.

www.ingramcontent.com/pod-product-compliance
Lightning Source LLC
Chambersburg PA
CBHW071441130726
47997CB00006B/2178